Reader Praise for
Melody Carlson's Diary of Teenage Girl Series

"I just want to say that your stories really inspired me and totally gave me a new relationship with God. Thank you so much!"

"   eries and
h

"   n impact
o

"   words in
y   to God.
Y

"   ed me."

"   connect
v   girls feel
t   changed
r

Praise for
Previous Melody Carlson Titles

"Melody Carlson's style is mature and bitingly funny, and her gift for connecting our heart to the character's plight also connects us to the complicated human condition and our need for one another."

—PATRICIA HICKMAN, best-selling author
of *Fallen Angels* and *Sandpebbles*

"Melody Carlson never fails to drag us out of our Christian easy chairs and right into the coals of the confusing culture in which we all find ourselves. She never fails to reveal that place of compassion within each of us. Excellent."

—LISA SAMSON, author of *The Church Ladies*
and *Tiger Lillie*

"Melody brings a rich authenticity to her stories. She shows us ourselves and others in ways we hadn't clearly seen before. Reading a novel by Melody is like taking a journey into hidden places of the soul and finding that God is already there."

—ROBIN JONES GUNN, best-selling author
of *Sisterchicks on the Loose!*

OTHER BOOKS FOR TEENS BY MELODY CARLSON

Diary of a Teenage Girl series
TrueColors series
Degrees of Betrayal series
Degrees of Guilt series
Letters from God for Teens
Piercing Proverbs

IRELAND

notes from a spinning planet

IRELAND

a novel

Melody Carlson

WATERBROOK
PRESS

Notes from a Spinning Planet—Ireland
Published by WaterBrook Press
12265 Oracle Boulevard, Suite 200
Colorado Springs, Colorado 80921
A division of Random House Inc.

10-Digit ISBN: 1-4000-7144-5
13-Digit ISBN: 978-1-4000-7144-9

Library of Congress Cataloging-in-Publication Data
Carlson, Melody.
   Notes from a spinning planet—Ireland / Melody Carlson.—1st ed.
       p. cm.
   Summary: Traveling in Ireland with her journalist aunt and the charming Ryan, her aunt's godson, nineteen-year-old Maddie unearths the secret behind an Irish Republican Army bombing decades earlier and the impact it has had on Ryan's and Aunt Sid's lives.
       ISBN-13: 978-1-4000-7144-9 (pbk.)
       ISBN-10: 1-4000-7144-5 (pbk.)
       1. Northern Ireland—Juvenile fiction. [1. Northern Ireland—Fiction. 2. Irish Republican Army—Fiction. 3. Aunts—Fiction. 4. Christian life—Fiction. 5. Voyages and travels—Fiction.] I. Title.
   PZ7.C216637Not 2006
   [Fic]—dc22

                                                            2006025753

Printed in the United States of America
2006—First Edition

10 9 8 7 6 5 4 3 2 1

One

It's pretty humiliating to admit, but I've never flown in a plane before today. Consequently, I haven't been out of the country either. Wait a minute, there was that one memorable car trip to Vancouver, BC, when I was eight and plagued with this unfortunate case of motion sickness that left our car smelling like sour milk for several months afterward. Other than that, the sad truth is that I've been *stuck on the farm*. Seriously, my parents actually run a small farm in Washington State. And some of my closest friends have been known to call me "the country bumpkin," which I totally detest. Although I suppose it fits.

Three of these same close friends begged me to join them for a European trip after high-school graduation a year ago, but my parents couldn't exactly afford such an "extravagance." Plus I had already promised Dad I'd help him get the hay in, since my older brother, Jake, had just gone into the air force. As a result I was forced to pass on what seemed a once-in-a-lifetime opportunity. My best friend, Katie, rubbed it in nicely by sending me a postcard from Paris—my absolute dream destination. Showing not even an ounce of compassion, she wrote, "Poor Madison, our country bumpkin, stuck on the farm again…" In Katie's defense (and trust me, she needed it), she was pretty bummed that I wasn't able to go with them, since it kind of made her the odd girl out. Even so, she wasn't nearly as bummed as I was, literally picking hayseeds from my hair as I studied the swanky photo of the Eiffel Tower against a Parisian blue sky. It all seemed totally unfair.

So wouldn't you think I'd be feeling pretty jazzed right now? I mean, just one year later I'm actually flying high over the Atlantic Ocean! And yet, here I am clinging to these wimpy armrests in white-knuckled terror. Why on earth did I ever agree to climb aboard this never-ending roller coaster?

"It's just a little turbulence," my aunt assures me for like the umpteenth time. I think I can hear a little impatience in her voice.

"Yeah, right." I nod and slowly release my death grip, trying to act like everything's cool. "So, will it be like this *all* the way across the ocean?"

"You just never know, Maddie." Her blue eyes glint with a teasing look. "It might get even worse."

"Really?" My fingernails start to dig into the armrests again.

Now she just laughs. "I doubt it. Just jerking your chain, sweetie. *Relax.*"

"Thanks a lot."

"Remember the deep breathing?"

I frown at her and then for her benefit exhale loudly.

"Just try not to think about it so much."

"Like him?" I nod to where Ryan is blissfully snoozing across the aisle from us like he hasn't a care in the world.

She laughs. "Yeah, I think that kid could sleep through a hurricane."

"We're not going to fly through one, are we?"

She shakes her head, then turns back to the *People* magazine I picked up at the airport, the same rag mag my journalist aunt made fun of earlier and can't put down now. Okay, it's not exactly intellectual, but I like to keep up on current events, plus there was a good article on Orlando Bloom. But I already studied it from cover to cover and am now wishing I hadn't packed my new novel in my checked bag. To help distract myself from my newly discovered flying phobia, I take advantage of Ryan's unconscious state to candidly check this guy out. I'm still trying not to feel too aggravated over his intrusion into *my* travel plans. This trip to Ireland was originally just going to be my aunt and me.

Anyway, I check him out and decide he's not too bad looking, although his sandy brown hair could use a cut or maybe just a comb. And I'm sure he'd be a lot more attractive if he closed his gaping mouth. If I'm not mistaken, there's a drop of saliva trickling down the left side of his chin, which makes me notice he could also use a shave.

Okay, it's not like I've never seen Ryan McIntire before. But it's been quite a while. We first met when we were about eleven or twelve, one summer when I got to spend an entire week at my aunt Sid's house in Seattle. That was back when Ryan didn't have whiskers on his chin and I still thought boys had cooties. For some reason my aunt thought it was a splendid idea to take us to the zoo together, but as I recall, I spent most of the day trying to avoid this weird kid who acted more like a resident of the zoo than merely a visitor. I suppose he's grown up a lot since then.

Ryan is my aunt's godson. His mom, Danielle, was Sid's best friend since kindergarten, but Danielle died last winter after a long bout with breast cancer. I'm suspecting that's the main reason Sid invited Ryan to join us on this trip at what seemed like the last minute. Fortunately for him, he already had a passport. Mine hadn't arrived yet, and I'd started to worry that I was about to be left behind once again.

"You don't mind, do you?" my aunt said just a few days ago, right after she'd cheerfully informed me that we were going to be a threesome.

"No, of course not," I said quickly, hiding my disappointment. Oh sure, I did feel sorry for Ryan. Who wouldn't? I can't imagine what it would feel like to lose my mother. But having him join us seemed to change everything.

"You see, Ryan's dad was from Ireland," she explained. "And Ryan and I were just talking about his heritage, and it suddenly occurred to me that I should invite him to come with us. He can look into his Irish roots while we're there. You two always got along fairly well, Madison. And he's grown up into a really nice young man. You guys might actually have some things in common now. Besides that, he can help carry our luggage."

She was starting to sound almost apologetic, so I decided I'd better get on board with this new twist in the plot—especially considering she was footing the bill for all my travel expenses. "Sounds great," I told her. "I can't wait to see him again." Okay, that was a slight exaggeration. But I'm sure it made her happy. And I did put on a good show this morning when I met the two of them at the airport.

Mom, who had driven me to Sea-Tac, was busy catching up with Sid and carefully going over our itinerary for like the hundredth time. Seriously, what does she think is going to happen to me once I'm out of her sight? Hijacking? Kidnapping? Forced slavery? And even if something should go wrong, how's it going to help matters if she knows where we are when it does? *Get real, Mom.*

"Wanna grab a coffee?" Ryan asked me just as my mom started to grill me about whether I'd forgotten anything important. I almost expected her to ask if I was wearing clean underwear just in case the plane crashed. Anyway, I was grateful to Ryan for providing me with this much-needed escape. Seriously, it's like my mom thinks I'm about eight years old sometimes. I'm surprised she didn't pin my name to my jacket.

We left our bags for the two women to "attend" since we'd already been informed numerous times by the PA system that "any luggage or personal items left unattended should be reported and confiscated…" And what then? Would the airport personnel take them out back and blow them up? Anyway, happy for this reprieve, I followed Ryan, who seemed to know where he was going, and we ended up at a Starbucks. Who knew they had Starbucks in airports? Well, everyone besides me, I suppose.

"This'll go fast," he assured me when he noticed how I was frowning at the long line ahead of us. "And it'll be worth it since it's way better than the stuff they serve on the plane."

"So you've flown before?" Okay, as soon as the words were out, I knew how totally lame I sounded. Like maybe I should get the words *country bumpkin* stamped across my forehead. *Smooth, Madison.*

"Yeah, sure." Fortunately he didn't inquire about my own embarrassing traveler's status.

"So, are you in college now?" I asked, trying to switch the subject so I wouldn't seem too pathetic.

"Yeah, I'll be a junior this fall."

I nodded. "Oh, that's right. You're a year older than me, aren't you?"

"I'll be twenty-one in November."

"Cool."

"How about you? Sid said you're in community college. How's that going?"

I shrugged. "It's okay. But I'll probably transfer to a bigger school sometime next year."

"That's cool."

"What's your major?"

"I'm not really sure yet." Then he got this blank kind of look, like he had left the planet or was thinking about something else, something a whole lot more interesting than me. So I sort of looked away like I was totally absorbed by the specials list up by the cashier: "Hazelnut Mocha, Caramel and Cream, Cinnamon Hottie Latte." Who comes up with these things?

"Sorry."

"Huh?" I looked back at Ryan.

"I guess I was spacing out on you. Kind of like a flashback, you know? Or maybe it was déjà vu. I'm not really sure what the difference is."

"Well, a flashback is when you remember something that *really* happened before," I told him, "and déjà vu is when you see something that *feels* like it happened before but never really did, unless it was in your imagination or a dream or something."

"Wow, are you some kind of word expert?"

"Not really. But I am into writing. I guess I sort of take after my aunt in that area. I think I'll probably major in journalism, like she did."

"It was cool of her to invite us to come on this trip with her," he said as we moved forward in the line, like about three and a half inches. "I mean, since she's really on assignment. But I've always wanted to go to Ireland."

"Yeah. I've always wanted to go *anywhere*. I've been so jazzed these past couple of months. Even right now I can hardly believe I'm really doing this."

And now, as I sit here trying to do the deep-breathing and calming exercises that Sid showed me shortly after takeoff and as the turbulence starts getting seriously bad, I still can't believe it. I mean, *What was I thinking?*

TWO

Sid made me promise to keep a travel journal on this trip. "It'll be something you can look back on when you're an old lady like me," she told me as she handed me this dark brown leather-covered book that's almost too cool to write in. The paper feels as smooth as silk.

"No problem," I assured her. "You know how I love to write anyway. And besides, you're *not* an old lady." Okay, I'm not really sure how old she is, but since she's my dad's baby sister, I've always figured that she's way younger than him. Although he is in his fifties, which actually sounds fairly old. But the thing about Sid is that she's really stylish. With her shoulder-length blond hair and slim figure, I'm guessing she could be in her late thirties or maybe even forty. The weird thing is she's never been married—weird because she's really good-looking and weird because I think she's pretty cool, for an older person anyway.

Of course, she appreciated my compliment. "Keep up the flattery, Maddie, and I'll take you on all my research trips," she promised. "Maybe you can be my new assistant."

Well, I'm not so sure I want to take any more flying trips. I try to distract myself from the nonstop turbulence by writing in my journal, although some of the words seem to be leaping from the page just now. So far I've filled about four pages, front and back. At this rate, I may need a new book by the time we land in Shannon—that's if we ever do. I don't know how everyone else can sleep with this plane rocking and rolling its way to the other side of the planet.

Sid said we're flying over the polar icecap to save time. And now I can't help but wonder how cold it might be down there and what would happen if we crash-landed. Would we even survive the impact? And if we did, would we survive the freezing cold temperatures and polar bears? And if we did survive that, would we ever be found? Would our cell phones work? Would desperate and starving passengers eventually resort to cannibalism to stay alive? I saw a movie about that once—a bunch of South American soccer players survived after a crash by eating their friends who died. Maybe I should've worn heavy socks and boots instead of these flimsy flip-flops, which Katie assured me would be perfect for getting through the security gates without a hitch. *Thanks, Katie!*

I pause from my writing as I think about my best friend. Just yesterday she informed me that she thinks she'll be engaged before I get back. Okay, this seems totally crazy to me. And I told her so. Like who gets engaged at nineteen? But she told me she's in love, and he's *the one,* and she knows it's the right thing to do. They only met last fall—at Washington State University, of course. "That's what comes from going away to school," my mom told me after I shared Katie's surprising news.

Maybe Mom's right. My parents tempted me into staying home with the offer of a new, slightly used car. They figured it wouldn't hurt me or my college account to go to the local community college for my first two years of higher education. Yeah, right—higher than what? But so far, unlike Katie, I haven't met anyone I'm even remotely interested in. Honestly, these guys all seem to be a bunch of country bumpkins, just like me. I suppose that's due to the agricultural program the school is known for. But, honestly, why would anyone in his right mind go to college to learn how to be a farmer? Besides my dad, that is. He likes to remind me of this whenever I complain about school.

Honestly, if I didn't like my car so much (it's a 2004 Honda Accord), I'd probably back out of the whole deal and go away to school like Katie. But I guess one more year at home won't kill me. To be honest, I wouldn't mind being home right now, stuck on the farm. It would be preferable to crash-landing in the Arctic Circle and being cannibalized by my fellow passengers.

"You gonna eat that?"

I turn around and look across the aisle at Ryan. He's pointing to the chocolate-chip cookie on my food tray, still in its package. "Want it?" I hold it out to him.

"Sure." He grins. "Who knows when lunch'll be served?"

I glance at my watch. According to Pacific time, it's about noon now, and I'm thinking maybe I should've held on to that cookie. "When do we adjust the time on our watches?" I ask.

"Whenever you want," he says as he eats the cookie in two quick bites. "I already changed mine." He brushes cookie crumbs from the front of his T-shirt, then glances at his watch. "Right now it's almost eight o'clock at night in Ireland." He grins.

"Seriously? It's night there already?" I try to absorb this fact. "So what time will it be when we finally land?"

"Around eight in the morning, *tomorrow,* which will then be today."

"That's so weird. I mean, we left a little after eight this morning. It's like it takes twenty-four hours to get there."

"Not really. Remember, we lose eight hours because of the time zones."

I try to do the clock math in my head, but somehow I keep messing it up. I've never been a real numbers person. Finally I just change my watch and try to convince myself that, despite the fact I haven't even had lunch, it's already nighttime now. Pretty bizarre.

Following what I know has been the longest day of my entire life, we land in Shannon. While everyone else on the darkened plane pretty much snoozed the past several hours, I remained wide awake with my imagination running wild the whole time. I might've actually dozed off a couple of times, but wild dreams (or turbulence-induced hallucinations) of frozen tundra and hungry polar bears quickly brought me back to my senses. Consequently, I'm feeling totally wiped out now. To use an old cliché, which is something a good writer would never do, I feel like something the cat dragged in. Sorry, but that's the best description I can come up with in my somewhat brain-dead condition. My hair feels skanky, my teeth are wearing furry sweaters, and my breath must be toxic. Somehow I lost the packet of hygiene goodies that the flight attendants distributed at the start of this flight, and now I discover there was a toothbrush and toothpaste in the neat little plastic pack.

At the moment, Ryan and I are sitting in this big, sparse holding area of the Shannon airport. We actually landed in Dublin first, and I thought that was the end of our journey. But we stayed on the plane, and Sid explained that we still had one more short flight. Finally, about an hour and a half later, we got off the plane. I restrained myself from falling down and kissing the earth, but seriously, it felt so good to have my feet on solid ground again. I can't even begin to think what I'll do when it's time to go home.

We had just started to go through customs when Sid was approached by this guy in a uniform. He told us she'd be right back, but it's been nearly an hour now, and I'm starting to get worried. What if they kidnapped her? Maybe my mom was right to be so cautious and worried about our whereabouts during this trip. I'm tempted to call Mom on my cell phone right now—to tell her we're barely here and Aunt Sid has gone missing.

"Your phone is just for emergencies," Dad sternly told me before I left this morning—or was that yesterday morning? Who knows? But he was pretty worried that international calls would break the bank. So I resist the urge.

"Shouldn't Sid be back by now?" I ask Ryan, pretending not to be nervous.

He just shrugs like it's no big deal, but I think I see a trace of worry in his eyes too.

"Who's she talking to anyway?"

"Just some official dude."

"I know it's some official dude," I say in a less-than-patient tone. "I saw the uniform. But who was it? And why did he want Sid?"

He shrugs again, and maybe it's my general fatigue, but his nonchalance is really starting to irritate me. Besides that, I'm hungry. And, unlike the American airport we departed from like, a hundred years ago, this part of the terminal doesn't seem to have any food kiosks or restaurants. There are a couple of vending machines, but since we don't have any euros yet, we're out of luck.

"Do you think we're *really* in Ireland?" I ask Ryan. He gives me this kind of *duh* look. Before I can say anything else stupid, I see Sid hurrying back toward us.

"Everything okay?" I ask as I get up to meet her.

"Yeah." She nods. "Just had to answer some questions."

"Questions?"

"I guess my name was on some kind of list, and they wanted to find out—"

"What kind of list?" I ask.

Sid is already collecting her baggage. "It's just old stuff that has to do with politics and when I was here before…not terribly important," she says. "Let's get you guys through customs now. We're burning daylight here."

So Ryan and I trudge along after her. I partially carry and partially drag my stuff toward the customs counter as I wonder what the showers are like in Ireland. I'm in serious need.

To my dismay, it seems the customs guys are really interested in the three of us. They make us open all our bags. And then, wearing these vinyl gloves, they search through everything, including my underwear, which I find just a tad bit embarrassing since I've never been one to buy the really fashionable stuff like my friend Katie goes for. But what's up with this anyway? Like who do they think we are? International smugglers or spies? Drug transporters? They finally seem satisfied that we're not any of those things, and after I push my stuff back into the bag and barely get the zipper closed, we head over to another counter to exchange some American money for euros, which really seems like a ripoff since they take far more dollars than I get back. I get about fifteen in exchange for a twenty.

"What was that all about?" I ask my aunt as we wait for Ryan. "I mean, the customs guys. It's like they thought we were serious trouble or something."

She just smiled. "It has to do with old things, Maddie. I'll explain later."

Okay, this makes me really curious. Like what was my aunt involved in here in Ireland? What makes her the kind of person who would be detained in customs? A woman of international interest? But I quickly forget these questions as we pile into a shuttle bus, and it speeds down the wrong side of the road. It drops us at the rental-car place just outside of the airport, and it takes about thirty minutes for Sid to fill out the paperwork there so she can rent this funny little vanlike car with the steering wheel on the right. Sure feels like the wrong side to me.

"Do you know how to drive this thing?" I ask her as we pile our stuff into the hatchback.

"It's been a while," she admits. "But it's probably like riding a bike."

Ryan offers to help read the map, and I opt for the backseat, thinking maybe I'll get to nap as Sid drives us to this place she's been raving about. Apparently it will take us a few hours to get there, which means I might actually catch some z's. However, when my aunt nearly collides head-on with a large delivery truck, I quickly discover that napping will be a challenge.

"The *other* way," Ryan yells.

We're driving in some kind of a circle thing, and the cars are all honking, and she's backing up and actually swearing. I don't think I've ever heard my aunt use bad language before, and it makes me even more worried.

"I'm sorry," she says when she finally gets back into the circle, going the right way now. I lean over the back of the front seat and just shake my head as she drives around this circle a couple of times.

"Where are we going?" I ask.

"I missed the exit on the roundabout," she says.

"*That* one!" yells Ryan.

"Right."

"No, *left*!"

"Yeah, yeah," she says as she turns left. "I know, I know."

And that's how it goes until we are finally out of the city. But after this the roads, which I thought were rather narrow before, get really, really narrow. I mean, like about the width of a single-car-driveway narrow, so narrow that someone has to pull over, practically off the road, when there's two-way traffic, which fortunately doesn't happen much.

I find that I am gripping the back of Ryan's seat and practically holding my breath as we hurtle down the wrong side of the road

at what looks like more than eighty-five kilometers on the speed-
ometer! How does that translate into miles? Worse than this is that
other vehicles, which seem to be going even faster, are heading
straight toward us, like it's inevitable we will soon end up in a head-
on crash, and I'm certain this tinny little car will not hold up. I
wonder if it's ever been crash tested. Does it even have airbags? I
think I might actually pass out.

"Where are we going?" I finally manage to gasp after Sid nar-
rowly misses a sports car.

"We're heading up to Galway," Sid tells me.

"How long will that take?" I ask, feeling more and more like
the brat in the backseat who keeps whining, "Are we there yet?"
But I'm desperate.

"Looks like about half an hour," Ryan informs me as he peers
at the map.

"We'll stop for a bite to eat there," Sid says. "Then it's on to
Connemara."

"What's that?"

"Our final destination…well, at least for a few days."

"Oh." Okay, I really want to ask how much longer it will take
to get to Connemara, but I know I already sound like a pest. Better to just shut up and write in my journal. Good thing I don't get
carsick anymore.

Before long the traffic gets thicker, and it appears we're getting
close to Galway. Or so I assume. I don't want to ask, don't want to
sound as lame as I feel.

Fortunately, Sid seems to know where she's going as she turns
into the next roundabout, and before long she is parking along a
city street. "Here we are," she announces happily. "Now let's see if
Fionna's is still here."

"Who's Fionna?" I ask as I climb from the car and enjoy a good
stretch. I am so stiff from sitting and sitting and sitting that I'm not
even sure I can walk very well.

"It's a restaurant where Danielle and I ate a couple of times,
back in the dark ages when we were just kids."

I recall hearing about how my aunt and Danielle spent a year
in Ireland when they were in college, but I've never really asked
about it before. Never really thought about it.

"So what brought you guys over here in the first place?" I ask
as we walk along a cobblestone sidewalk that looks really old. In
fact, as I look at the buildings, I realize that everything here looks
pretty old. We're walking down this alleylike street with colorful
flags and banners flapping in the breeze, and there are street ven-
dors everywhere, as well as musicians, and I can smell something
really delicious cooking. It feels almost like a carnival, and I suddenly am totally invigorated, almost forgetting how long I've been
sleep deprived and how stiff I am. I hear a street vendor calling out
in a thick Irish accent, and it hits me—I really am in a different
country! I am halfway around the planet. *I am in Ireland!*

"Danielle and I came here on a goodwill mission," my aunt
begins, then stops suddenly, pointing across the street. "Look, it's
still there! Fionna's!"

We hurry across the street and get seated at a small bistro-style table outside, and Sid begins telling us how she and Danielle came over here when Ireland was a dangerous place, during what she calls "the troubles."

Three

I vaguely remember hearing about your trip to Ireland," I tell Sid. "I mean, I know you spent some time here, but I just assumed it was for fun."

She sort of laughs. "Well, parts of it were fun. I'll admit that. But parts of it were truly sad. It was a difficult time. Danielle and I first became aware of what was happening in Northern Ireland when we took this political-science class together," she begins. "We'd heard about the bombings, the senseless killings, all the hatred that seemed to be coming to a head between the Catholics and Protestants. It was in the news, but I suppose we hadn't paid too much attention. Anyway, it was 1975, and we were about your age—"

"Huh?" This doesn't make sense. Okay, I'm not that great at math, but 1975 sounds like a long time ago—like more than thirty years. "How old are you anyway, Aunt Sid?"

She laughs. "It's no secret, Maddie."

"She's around fifty," Ryan says bluntly. "Same age as my mom. Well, before she…you know…" Then he looks away, and I realize he's still dealing with his mom's death, and I wish I could say something to make it easier for him, but I have no idea what that would be. So I turn my attention back to my aunt, hopeful we'll move our conversation on to a happier subject.

"No way do you look like you're fifty!"

She smiles and pats my hand. "Like I said, Maddie, you keep this up, and I'll keep you around. Turning fifty wasn't exactly a piece of cake for me."

"So you guys came over here like thirty years ago?" I try to absorb these two facts: (1) my aunt's that old, and (2) she and Ryan's mom were right here in 1975.

"Anyway, Danielle and I were both in our second year of college when we took that political-science class from a professor who had just returned from Northern Ireland. The stories he told the class just broke our hearts. He showed us slides—these heartbreaking black-and-white photos of Irish children growing up in Northern Ireland among such hatred and violence and hopelessness. So by the end of our sophomore year, when this same professor put up a poster about an opportunity to help out at a summer camp that needed volunteers, both Danielle and I signed right up."

"Where was the camp located?" I ask.

"On an old estate about thirty miles out of Belfast. A family donated this gorgeous piece of property with the goal of uniting Protestant and Catholic children in a camplike atmosphere. It was called a peace camp. They hoped it would provide a means for kids to learn to accept their religious and political differences before they became too biased."

"Cool idea," I tell her. "Did it work?"

"It seemed to. I mean, the campers arrived with some obvious problems and prejudices, but after they started having fun and act-ing like regular kids, they seemed to almost forget their differences. At least while they were there. Who knows what happened after they went home." She pauses as the waitress comes to take our order.

"Of course, those children are all grownups now," she contin-ues. "Probably in their thirties and forties." She shakes her head and sighs as if this is hard to believe.

"I wonder how it affected their lives."

"Well, that's exactly why I'm here, Maddie. My assignment is to write a follow-up article about the peace-camp kids we worked with thirty years ago. I've contacted some former campers who agreed to interviews. And I've heard that one was actually involved in the Good Friday Agreement."

"What's that?" I ask as I set aside the menu.

"That's when the IRA agreed to disarm," Ryan informs me, "several years ago. It was a huge thing for Northern Ireland. A lot of people thought it wouldn't work, and it was a little rough at first. But the bombings and shootings have really gone down since then—on both sides."

I glance at him, curious as to how he knows so much about this. I mean, I don't exactly live under a stone, and I do know that the IRA stands for the Irish Republican Army, and I think they formed to drive the British Protestants out of Ireland, or something to that effect.

"It really was a monumental step for unity in Ireland," says Sid. "Of course, the Good Friday Agreement hasn't solved all their problems, but it was a big shift toward peace."

"I don't like to sound ignorant," I admit, "but I guess I don't know that much about all of this. Like how it all started or why. Well, other than the fact that Catholics and Protestants seem to hate each other. But I don't really get that. I mean, aren't they both supposed to be Christians?"

"It's pretty complicated," says Sid. "And it goes back hundreds of years. In a nutshell, it has to do with Northern Ireland wanting independence from Britain, wanting to be reunited with the Republic of Ireland."

"The reason the religious aspect is messy is because most of the Irish are Catholics, and most of the British are Protestants," says Ryan. "And the history of Catholics and Protestants, particularly on this side of the globe, is that they don't get along. So this whole Irish-independence thing starts to look like a religious war too."

"Sort of like two cultures colliding, and neither one of them wants to accept the other," continues Sid.

"Why don't the British just go back to Britain?" I ask.

"That would sure make the Irish happy," says Ryan.

Sid kind of laughs. "Yeah, if only it were that simple. But, unfortunately, it involves things like money and land and pride."

"But it seems like the two Irelands should be reunited," I protest, feeling sorry that the country has been divided like this. "It seems wrong that they've been split apart if they're both really Irish."

"Keep in mind that a lot of British people live in Northern Ireland," explains Sid. "Some have been here for generations. They think of it as their home, and it's not like they're going to just pack up and leave."

"Why can't they stay but let Northern Ireland be reunited with the rest of Ireland?"

"That's sort of like asking why the Native Americans can't have North Dakota back," says Ryan.

"Huh?"

"In other words, it's complicated," says Sid.

"Well, I don't see why people can't just get along," I say as the waitress brings our drinks.

To my relief, Sid changes the subject by telling us a little more about where we're going to be staying today.

"Connemara is one of the most untouched regions of Ireland," she explains, sounding a bit like a travel brochure. "The town we'll stay in is called Clifden, and it's by the sea. Really pretty and quaint. I've booked us a bed-and-breakfast for three nights. It's in one of the oldest buildings and in the center of town."

"Sounds nice," I say as I take a sip of what is supposed to be Coke, although I'm skeptical.

"One of the men I need to interview tomorrow lives north of Clifden," she continues. "I'm not sure how long it will take, but I figure you two can kick around town while I get my interview. Maybe you can rent some bikes and see the countryside, or take a ferry tour to one of the islands, or just hang out and do some shopping."

"Or maybe take a nice long nap." I yawn as I look down the narrow street we're sitting beside, and I'm struck once again by the fact I am really in a foreign country. "These old buildings are so cool," I say as I study the stone structure directly across from us.

The large double doors are painted bright blue, as are the flower boxes, which overflow with red geraniums and lots of other bright blooms that hang down several feet.

I point to the carved sign over the door that reads *Céad Míle Fáilte*. "What do you think that means?" I ask my aunt.

"As I recall, it's 'welcome.' "

"That's a pub," Ryan informs me.

"A pub?" I ask. "It looks more like a hotel to me."

"He's right," says Sid. "It is a pub. But pubs in Ireland aren't like the ones at home."

"How's that?"

"Well, most of them are more of a social place. They serve food and often have live music or some other form of entertainment. And here's the kicker: unlike back home, they allow children inside. It's kind of a family place, really."

"Seriously?" I look back across the street and have to admit that it does look like a pleasant enough place, but even so, I have my doubts about children in drinking establishments. "They really let little kids go into the bars here?"

"They're not *bars,* Maddie. *Pubs.* Of course, kids come with their parents, and they don't serve juveniles alcohol."

"But the drinking age is lower here," says Ryan.

"How low?" I ask.

"Eighteen." He grins like he's pleased by this fact.

Now I'm not too sure what I think about that. I mean, it's not like I haven't tasted alcohol before, but it's not something I'm into. That's partly because I'm a Christian and partly because my parents, who are pretty conservative, made me promise when I was about thirteen that I wouldn't drink either. Sure, I've broken that promise a couple of times, but I was always sorry afterward. Anyway, I know my parents wouldn't be too thrilled if they discovered I was over here partying in Ireland. But I must admit the idea of being "legal" is kind of interesting too.

Our food comes, and I am pleasantly surprised to discover it's really delicious. I mean, it's only a ham sandwich and fries (or what they call chips), but everything about it is really superb. "I didn't know they had such good food in Ireland," I say as we're finishing up.

"Why wouldn't they?" asks Sid as she puts her credit card with the bill.

"Well, my friend Katie said that English food is pretty disappointing."

"This is *not* England." Sid winks at me. "And don't you forget it."

"Aye, lassie," says Ryan, putting on a pretty good Irish accent. "We Irish dinna take kindly to being confused with those Brits across the way."

"That's pretty good," I tell him. "But then again, you do have Irish roots. It probably comes naturally to you."

Of course, this only encourages him, and he continues with his Irish chitchat as we walk back to the car. Soon we are on our way again. I'm not sure if it's the food or the driving or just the excitement of being here, but despite my lack of sleep, I am feeling wide awake and enthused about everything.

"This is so incredibly beautiful," I say once we're out of town and driving through some very lush, green countryside.

"It's not all that different from some places in Washington State," observes my aunt.

"Maybe," I reply, "but the houses and everything look so much older and more charming."

"That's true," she says. "They definitely have lots more history. But their climate is very similar to the Northwest, although I believe they get more rain."

"More rain?" I question this. "I didn't think anyone got more rain than western Washington."

"Trust me," says my aunt. "Ireland does."

"In fact, it looks like we're going to get rained on up ahead," says Ryan.

Sure enough, in about five minutes the sky grows seriously dark, and we are driving through a deluge.

"Must be how it stays so green," I say as I watch the wiper blades swiping furiously back and forth and hope our little car won't hydroplane off the road.

"Connemara is one of the wettest parts of Ireland," says my aunt. "I think I read that some parts of this peninsula can get up to three hundred inches of rain a year."

"Three hundred inches?" I echo with disbelief.

"I think we must be driving through that part right now." Ryan actually ducks as a big truck whooshes perilously close to us (on the right side of the road, which still seems totally freaky to me), and as it goes by—so near that I think we're going to scrape sides—it pushes a wave of water over our car, and it feels like we're riding in a submarine.

Sid slows down, and I think we all take a collective deep breath. "Driving around here can be a little unnerving sometimes," she finally says.

"Do you want us to help out?" I offer, not sure that I'd really be much help. I probably would've totally lost it back there with the truck.

"I wish," she says. "But you have to be twenty-five to drive a rental car over here."

"Too bad," I say, feeling relieved.

"Aye, lassie," says Ryan, "ya can drink, but ya canna drive."

After about ten minutes of intermittent showers, the rain seems to be letting up some, and Ryan actually spots a gorgeous double rainbow off to our left.

"That must be our promise for a good visit," says my aunt. Then she puts on the brakes so quickly that I actually grab the seat in fear.

When I look out the front window to see why she's stopping, I'm surprised to see a small herd of sheep meandering across the road. They have curly wool that resembles dreadlocks, long rounded horns, and cute dark faces.

"I think those are Scotch Blackface sheep," I announce, pleased that I'm finally able to contribute something a tiny bit informative.

"How do you know *that*?" Ryan asks, like he thinks I shouldn't be breaking out of my role as village idiot just yet.

"For your information," I tell him in a Miss Know-It-All tone, "it just so happens that I raised sheep for 4-H, and I'm something of a sheep expert, thank you very much."

Fortunately, he laughs at this.

"In fact," I continue, "my dad was doing some online research about farming in Ireland last week. He told me that sheep are really big over here. Farmers raise them for their meat as well as their wool. In fact, I think he said there are actually more sheep than people."

"That sounds about right," says Sid as the last pair of straggler lambs finally make some quick leaps to get up and over the stone embankment. Most of the roads seem to be bordered with these stone walls. While they are pretty and kind of quaint, they do make the roads feel even narrower and tighter, and I'm sure they could do some serious damage to your car if you got too close, which seems like a very real possibility.

"Look at that thatched-roof cottage," I exclaim when I spot a very old-fashioned-looking house on the edge of the road. "Do they still use thatched roofing? Or is this just some kind of a tourist attraction?"

"They still use thatching in some of the older homes," says Sid as she slows down so we can have a better look. "I've heard that if the thatch is maintained, it can last for decades."

After about forty minutes of driving through some of the most beautiful countryside, we stop at a place that sells pottery and sweaters and other Irish items of interest. "This is kind of a tourist trap," my aunt explains. "But I could use a coffee."

So we get coffee and then wander around and look at the merchandise. My aunt finds a pitcher and bowl she decides she can't live without. Then we get back into the car and head on to Clifden.

It's about three o'clock when we reach our destination, and I immediately fall in love with this sweet little town. We climb out of the car into bright sunshine and clear blue skies, with the smell of freshly baked bread wafting over the sea air.

"This is awesome," I say to my aunt as I look around at the quaint little shops and stone buildings. "What a great place to stay!"

We check into our bed-and-breakfast and, thanks to Ryan, manage to lug all our bags up three flights of steep narrow stairs in only one trip. No elevator. The plan is for Sid and me to share a room. Naturally, Ryan gets his own, a much smaller one, and he gets to share a bathroom down the hall.

"Swanky," I say as we go into our room.

Sid laughs as she sets her carry-on bag on one of the beds. "It is rather pretty, isn't it?"

"Look at all these incredible antiques," I gush as I scope out our room, which I'm pleased to find has its own private bath, complete with an old-fashioned claw-foot tub. "My mom would go nuts over this place."

"Make sure you get some photos for her," Sid says as she unzips a bag and removes her camera.

"That's right," I say. "I should've been taking pictures all day today—the sheep, the rainbow, the thatched—"

"Don't worry," she assures me. "You'll have lots of photo ops here."

"Hey, check out this view," I say as I push back the lace curtains to spot a wide strip of blue water beyond the shorter buildings. "The ocean!"

Sid comes over and stands by me without saying anything.

"Isn't it gorgeous?"

But still she is silent. Finally I turn around to look at her, and to my shock there are tears running down her cheeks. And something tells me—maybe it's her expression—that these are not tears of happiness.

"Are you okay?" I ask.

She sniffs and turns away. "Yeah," she says in a gruff voice as she heads for the bathroom. "I'll be okay in a minute or two."

I follow her to the bathroom, watching as she blows her nose.

"What's wrong?" I ask.

She waves the tissue at me, as if she'd like to wave whatever it is away. "I just got, well, you know emotional. It's been so long since I've been back…and now all these memories are rushing at me, and…" Then she starts crying even harder. I go over to her, put my arms around her.

"Whatever it is," I assure her, "I'm sure it's going to be okay, Sid."

Okay, I'm not entirely convinced by my own words. In fact, I've never seen my aunt fall apart like this before. I mean, she's always seemed so strong. She's single, she's a career woman, she travels all over the world by herself—even to places like Iraq and Afghanistan. For the life of me, I cannot imagine what has caused her to come unglued like this.

"Maybe you're just tired," I finally say when I think she might be finished with her tears.

"Yes." She nods. "I am tired. Do you mind if I take a little nap?"

"Not at all," I say. "I'd take one too, but I'm so jazzed about being here that I doubt I can sleep just yet."

"Go ahead and ride the high," she says as she sits down on her bed and removes her shoes. "Explore the town and have some fun."

"Okay." I glance over to a table topped by a lace cloth, a china teapot, some teabags, and some kind of a device that Sid said was for heating water. "Maybe you could make some tea," I suggest meekly.

"Yes, that'll be nice. I'll have a little nap and then some tea afterward. Sounds perfect."

I reach for my bag. "I probably won't last too long out there," I say as I head for the door. "You sure you'll be okay?"

She looks up at me, smiling with sad eyes. "Please, don't worry about me, Maddie. I'm sorry about that little outburst. Honestly, I'll be just fine."

I nod as if I believe this and then open the door and slip out into the dimly lit hallway. But the truth is, I am seriously worried about my aunt. I don't know what's wrong, but I have a feeling it has to do with being here in Ireland—like maybe she's haunted by something from the past, something that just hit her when we were looking out at the ocean.

four

Clifden is so charming! It takes about half an hour to walk around its circumference, but I'm sure it would take a whole day just to look at all the shops. Right now, I'm just scoping it all out, although I did notice a sweater shop with a great-looking cardigan in the window. Mom gave me birthday money (early, since my birthday isn't until August) with very explicit directions. "I want you to get yourself a nice fisherman's-knit sweater, Maddie."

And so, after I've walked around the town and the wind starts to pick up, I decide to return to that sweater shop. Maybe I'll find something to wear over this thin T-shirt.

Before long, a helpful woman with white hair has located my size (which makes no sense to me because it's in metrics). But I try it on, and it seems to fit. She assures me that it looks lovely, plus it's warm, so I agree to purchase it.

"You could pass for a real Irish lassie," she says as she pats my naturally curly hair, which is curlier than ever thanks to the humidity here.

"Thank you," I tell her as I sign a traveler's check. I assume that's a compliment and take it as such. Then she asks where I'm from, and I tell her about our farm in Washington.

"I grew up on a farm too," she says, then counts out my

change, handing me a couple of euros as well as a bunch of coins I still haven't figured out.

"What kind of farming?" I ask as she removes the price tag from the sweater and hands it back to me.

"Oh, we grew a bit of everything back then, but my da is getting old now. He mostly raises sheep and has to have help with that." She points to my sweater. "Maybe some of Da's wool is in your sweater, dear."

I smile at her. "That'd be cool."

"Don't you mean warm?"

I laugh. "Yes, that's what I mean." Then I thank her and head back outside. I stand on the sidewalk for a moment just looking out at the town and wondering which way to go now. I'm not quite ready to return to the B&B and not sure if my aunt has had enough time to rest and recover from whatever she was bummed about. Besides, I'm still feeling a little giddy about being here, and it's kind of a high walking around this town all on my own. It's just so weird to think I'm so far from home and—

"Hey, Maddie!"

I turn and see Ryan waving at me from across the street. He's sitting at a wooden picnic table that's outside of what appears to be a pub. And in front of him is a tall glass of something brown. Although it's about the color of coffee, I suspect it's not. I suspect it's some kind of alcoholic drink. Maybe beer. And for some reason this just really throws me. Like what is Ryan doing? How is it okay for him to sit over there casually drinking a beer? And what will my aunt say about this when she finds out? But as I walk across the street, I remember the lower drinking age and decide to act non-chalant as I sit down and join him.

"How's it going?"

"Okay," he says. "Cool sweater. You look like you belong here now."

"Thanks."

"Want one?" he asks.

"One what?" I'm sure that sounds pretty lame, but it's a stall tactic on my part.

"A Guinness. Ireland's number one stout."

"What's a stout?"

"It's a dark beer. They roast the hops until they're dark brown and get kind of a coffee taste." He holds the glass out as if he's offering me a sample.

I bend over and take a sniff, then wrinkle my nose. "Yuck, smells like something my dad might feed the pigs."

He laughs and holds up his glass as if to make a toast. "Well, here's to the pigs then."

I study him as he takes a swig. "You really like that stuff?"

"Sure, why not?"

I shrug and look away.

"Does it bother you that I'm having a beer?" he asks. And the way he says this actually sounds like he cares.

I turn back and look at him. He does seem concerned. "I don't know."

"Because if it really disturbs you, well, I guess I could not—"

"No, no," I say, feeling kinda bad now. "You can drink if you want. It's not my place to tell you how to live your life. But what about Sid? Do you think she'll care?"

"I already talked to her about it."

"You did?"

"Yeah. I told her I planned to have a Guinness now and then. And she said as long as I didn't overdo it, she was fine."

"She was fine?" Now I'm not sure what to think about this. I mean, I realize that Sid is a lot different than my parents, but she *is* a Christian after all. And for some reason I guess I assumed that meant she'd have a problem with Ryan drinking. Apparently I was wrong.

"Yeah. She's pretty cool, Maddie."

Something about the way he says this makes me wonder if I should mention her little crying jag. If something really is wrong with Sid, I would want Ryan to be in the know. After all, he and Sid are pretty close too.

"Something weird happened at the inn," I begin tentatively.

"Weird?" He sets his glass down and frowns. "Weird as in creepy? Like you think the place might be haunted?" He laughs. "Actually, it's so old I suppose it might be."

I roll my eyes at him. "No. Nothing like that."

Then a waitress comes out. "Can I get a pint for you?"

I glance over at Ryan. "A *pint*?"

He holds up his glass. "*This* is called a pint."

I shake my head. "No, I definitely do not want a pint."

"What *would* you like?" she asks in a slightly impatient tone.

"What kind of pop do you have?"

"Pop?" She looks at me funny, then glances at Ryan as if she thinks he might be able to translate for me.

"Soda?" he offers. "A soft drink?"

Then she nods and says, "We have lemon, orange, cola, and—"

"Lemon," I say quickly, eager to get this over with.

"You need to learn the lingo," Ryan says after the waitress walks away. He holds up his glass and, talking like a schoolteacher, says, "This is a pint. It's filled with stout. And there's no such thing as pop, and—"

"That's enough!" I hold up my hand for him to stop. "No more language lessons, please!"

He laughs. "You really are fresh off the farm, aren't you, Maddie?"

I scowl at him. That's just the kind of joke I can live without.

"Okay, let's get back to weird."

"Huh?"

"You were saying how something weird happened at the inn."

"Oh, it was probably nothing," I say, now unsure as to whether I should continue.

"Come on," he urges. "What was weird?"

So I go ahead and spill the beans about Sid falling apart. "I mean, it wasn't like just a tear or two. She really came undone."

He considers this. "Did you ask her why?"

"No, not really. It seemed kind of like a private moment, you know, and I felt uncomfortable being there, like I was intruding."

He slowly nods and takes another sip, but I can tell by his

expression that he's thinking something specific, almost like he knows what was troubling my aunt. And then I remember his mom, and I feel absolutely horrible. Of course, it seems obvious now. Sid must've been remembering her best friend and how they'd come to Ireland together more than thirty years ago. And since he's not saying anything, I decide I should probably just get it out in the open.

"Do you think she was feeling bad about your mom?"

"Maybe."

Thankfully, the waitress comes out with a little green bottle that really doesn't look like pop (or a soda), but she sets it in front of me along with a small glass. "Thanks," I tell her as I pick up the roundish bottle and sniff at the opened top. Then I pour it into the glass and watch as it fizzes, and finally I take a tentative drink. It pretty much tastes like Sierra Mist, only not as sweet and more lemony. By the second sip, I think I might like this even better.

We both sit there in silence for a few minutes, just sipping our drinks and feeling, I think, uneasy. I'm desperately trying to think of something to say to Ryan, something that will move us past this thing about his mom. But I am coming up totally blank.

"It's hard moving on," he finally says. "I mean, my mom's been gone for almost four months, and I know I should be over it by now—"

"Why is that?" I say. "I mean, seriously, if *my* mom died, I doubt I'd ever get over it. Really, how does anyone get over something like that? Why should you feel like you have to move on?"

He seems honestly relieved at my admission. "Yeah, I guess you're right. Thanks, Maddie."

"The truth is, I'm not really that comfortable talking about this kind of thing. I mean, no one close to me has ever died. But I really feel for you, and I can't even begin to guess how you deal with this."

"No one ever does, not until it happens. Sometimes not even then."

"Sid told me that your dad died too, back when you were still pretty young."

"That wasn't the same," he says. "I was just a baby, and I don't even remember him."

"Still, it must be hard having both your parents gone."

He nods. "Yeah. I'm not really looking forward to holidays."

"Holidays with the family can be highly overrated."

He sorta laughs. "Well, maybe I'll connect with some of my dad's family while I'm here."

"Do you know any of them?"

He shakes his head. "Not at all. My dad was raised in the U.S. He came over here when he was about my age. That's when he met my mom."

"They met in Ireland?"

"Northern Ireland."

"That's kind of romantic."

He shrugged. "I guess."

"But then they went back to America?"

"Yes, after they got married. Then after I was born, he came back."

"Your dad came back here? To Ireland?"

"Yeah." He frowns now.

"Without you and your mom?"

"Pretty much. It was supposed to be a short trip, some kind of business…not something my mom ever talked about much."

"Oh."

"Then he never came back."

"He never came back? You mean he just abandoned you and your mom, Ryan? I thought he died."

"He did die. He died in Northern Ireland."

"Wow." I stare at him. "I had no idea."

"Well, it happened a long time ago. I don't think about it much. It's not really part of my life, you know. And then the thing with my mom… Well, it was a bigger deal losing her."

"Yeah." Still, I'm thinking it's strange that Ryan's dad returned to Ireland and died here. I want to ask him more about it, but he doesn't seem like he wants to go there right now. Since he's not even over his mom.

"So, do you think that's what Sid was dealing with this afternoon?" I'm trying to get the conversation back on track. "Just remembering your mom?"

"Maybe." But something in his expression doesn't convince me. Or maybe he's still thinking about his dad. I'm starting to see this guy is a bit of a mystery.

"Could it be something else?" I persist. "I mean, with Sid."

He takes another swig of beer. "Has Sid ever told you about Ian?"

"Ian?"

"Ian McMahan."

"Who's that?"

"She's never mentioned him?"

"No. But you've got me curious now. Who is Ian McMahan?"

"Well, maybe I shouldn't say anything if she—"

"No," I insist, "you brought up the name. Now you better tell me about this guy."

"Well, a few weeks before my mom died, Sid came over to stay with us and help out. Sometimes the two of them would stay up late, like when my mom was having a hard time sleeping and the meds weren't working. They talked a lot about Ireland and my mom and dad, and one time I overheard them talking about this Irish guy named Ian McMahan. It sounded like he was Sid's big true love. They met in Northern Ireland, but then something went wrong between them. I'm not sure what exactly. But I'm guessing by the way they talked that Ian McMahan broke Sid's heart."

"Oh." Oddly enough, this actually makes some sense. "You know, I've always wondered why Sid never married."

"Yeah, she's a pretty cool lady."

"It kinda makes sense that she could've been getting over some relationship that went sideways. But on the other hand, that was a long, long time ago."

"Some loves seem to last forever."

I think of my parents and wonder if maybe he's right.

"It makes sense that being here in Ireland might bring those memories back."

"Yeah. I bet you're right, Ryan. I'm just not sure what to do."

"I don't think you need to *do* anything." He takes his last drink and sets the empty pint down with a thud. "You know, besides being supportive and understanding and giving her space. Sometimes people just have to work out this kind of thing for themselves."

I'm about to ask if that's what he's doing. But he glances at his watch and suggests we should go.

I let a yawn escape. "Yeah. I feel like I'm about to crash myself. I must be running on fumes by now."

"That's what comes from staying awake during the flight." He picks up the bill.

"Wait," I say, reaching for my bag. "I'll get my own—"

"This one's on me, Maddie." He drops several euros on the table. "And maybe you'll let me buy you a Guinness before this trip is over."

I kind of roll my eyes at him. "Yeah, sure. I'll keep you posted on that one."

We find Sid in the lobby when we get back to the inn. She smiles when she sees us. "Hey, I thought you guys had run off without me."

"Just checking the place out," I tell her.

"Great sweater, Maddie. Did you get that in town?"

I do a little spin. "Yeah, I promised Mom I'd get a fisherman's knit. It's supposed to be her early birthday present to me. I wasn't too sure at first, but I think I actually like it. Plus it's warm."

"She looks like she belongs here now," says Ryan. "Guess I should go see if they have anything for guys there."

"They do," I tell him. "You should check it out."

"Anybody hungry?" asks Sid. "I heard there's a traditional Irish band playing at O'Hara's tonight."

"Where's that?" asks Ryan.

"Just a few blocks from here," she tells us. "I was going to run down to the market for a couple of things before it closes. Can you guys be ready to go to O'Hara's around seven then?"

"Sounds good to me," I tell her. "Maybe I can grab a quick nap in the meantime."

So it's all settled. Ryan decides to go to the store with her, but I trudge up the three flights of stairs and collapse on my bed. It seems like I've barely fallen asleep before my aunt is nudging me and saying it's time to go.

I feel like I'm in an Irish fog or suffering jet lag, but my head starts to clear as we walk the few blocks to O'Hara's. And once we're inside and seated, the sound of lively music and the smell of food wake me up even more.

"What time is it back home?" I ask as we peruse the menu.

"You're not supposed to think about that," says Ryan.

"That's right." Sid nods. "It won't mess with your head as much if you just go with the flow and forget what time it is back home."

"But what if I want to call my mom? I mean, I don't want to wake her up in the middle of the night." I point to the clock above the big rock fireplace. "So, do I go forward or backward?"

"They're eight hours *behind* Ireland," my aunt says as she sets her menu aside. "It's still morning there."

I try to process this and finally realize that my aunt and Ryan are probably right. I should forget about the time difference. And I really hadn't planned to call my mom anyway. "No news is good news," my no-nonsense dad had pointed out before I left. "If you call, it should be because something is wrong."

Once again our food is really good. I can't wait to tell Katie that she was so wrong about this. Of course, she never made it over to Ireland either. And like my aunt says, Ireland is *not* England. Although it does feel a little strange to be eating in a bar, or rather a *pub*. There are families with children here, though, and I realize it's really no big deal. While we're eating, the music really kicks in, and I discover that I like Irish music. It's lively, and the drums, which look like giant tambourines, sound very cool.

"I think I might have to get one of those drums," says Ryan while the band takes a break.

"Are you a musician?" I ask.

"I play guitar and bass," he says.

"Really?" For some reason this surprises me. "I play guitar too."

My aunt winks at me. "See, I told you that you guys have some things in common."

Then the waiter comes back to our table to see if we want anything else, and to my surprise, both my aunt and Ryan order a Guinness.

"And for the young lady?" The waiter looks at me.

"Nothing, thank you," I say crisply, not even trying to conceal my irritation.

My aunt jokes that she has to have at least one Irish beer while in Ireland. "When in Rome…," she says lightly and, I'm sure, for my benefit.

Even so, I find this whole thing unsettling. I'm not even sure why exactly. It's not like she's going to be driving or anything, not that one beer would impair her anyway. But, just the same, it bugs me. And it really bugs me that Ryan, who would be underage back home, can drink as much beer as he wants here, and it's totally legal.

When the band comes back to play, I find that I don't enjoy it nearly as much as before. It's like I'm mad or hurt or something, and even though I tell myself I'm being really silly about this whole beer thing, it's like I can't get over it. Not only that, but I feel like odd girl out. Not just because of the beer either. It's like both of them have these Irish connections—and secrets. And I'm just along for the ride. Extra baggage. But why?

I sit here watching them as they sip their stouts and chat as if it's no big deal. Part of me wants to just chill and accept this behavior, but the truth is, I think I'm judging them. Like I somehow think I'm better than they are because I'm *not* drinking. And yet I know that Christians aren't supposed to judge others.

Of course, this thought makes me face up to the fact that I haven't really been living much like a Christian myself lately. Being in college and helping on the farm, combined with all my Christian friends being away at school, well, it was easy to let things slide. Even so, I *know* I'm a Christian. Just not a very good one, I guess. But at least I'm not a boozing Christian!

Okay, I'm not really sure why I'm thinking about all this right now, but I guess I seem pretty checked out to Ryan and my aunt. Or maybe they checked out on me. Who knows? But when our evening at the pub finally comes to an end and we're walking back to the inn, I'm pretty quiet.

"You okay, Maddie?" My aunt wraps an arm around my shoulders and gives me a little squeeze.

"Yeah," I tell her. "Just tired, I guess."

"Not homesick?"

"No. Just exhausted." Okay, maybe that's not the whole truth, but it's not a lie either. And it's not like I'm going to admit that I feel left out right now.

"Well, I'm sure you'll sleep like a baby tonight."

As it turns out, she's right. I think I was asleep before I even hit the bed.

Five

"Y ou've got my cell phone number if you need me," my aunt says as she shoves her laptop and some papers into her briefcase.

"Yeah, yeah," I say from where I'm still lazing in bed. "Don't worry, Sid. Ryan and I will be okay on our own today. We won't get arrested or anything."

"That's so relieving, Maddie."

"Seriously, we'll be fine."

"If all goes well, I expect to be home around fiveish," she calls as she heads out the door. "You guys have fun, okay?"

"Okay," I call back as the door closes behind her. Then I flop back into my soft feather pillow and close my eyes and let out a great big sigh. *Jet lag.* I'm sure that has something to do with how I'm feeling right now. It's like I'm tired, but I'm not really sleepy. I'm kinda hungry, but I can't think of anything I want to eat. And my head feels sort of fuzzy, and my ears are still ringing from the flight.

Finally I force myself to get up. It's only eight and a lot earlier than I'd normally get up during summer break. That is, unless my dad's after me to help with something like haying. Then it's the crack of dawn or sooner.

This room doesn't have a TV, and while that's kind of refreshing and surprisingly peaceful, I still feel curious about what's going on in the bigger world. My mom usually has a news show going in the morning, and it seems I pick up on the latest by some sort of osmosis. Eventually I force myself into the bathroom and turn on the shower. Everything in here is very old, with exposed painted pipes and tiles that look ancient. The water comes out in a slow dribble, but at least it's hot. Since there's no hurry, I figure a slow, drippy, hot shower is better than nothing. It does feel good to get rid of yesterday's flight grime.

By the time I get dressed and make it downstairs, Ryan is sitting like a king at the head of a long table. His plate is loaded with bacon and eggs and some good-looking pastries.

"Leave any for me?"

"This is seconds for me, and I'm actually considering thirds," he says as he takes a bite of bacon. "You better hurry and get some while you can."

Fortunately there is plenty of food left. And despite my earlier feeling of not being hungry, I heap my plate and manage to eat almost all of it.

"I was thinking about renting a bike this morning," he informs me as we're both finishing up, "and then riding over to where the ferry leaves for Inishbofin."

"Inish what?"

"Inishbofin." He holds up a brochure. "Apparently it's an island. They have ferries that go out several times a day. You wanna give it a try?"

"Sure." I push my empty plate aside and study the brochure. It looks like a pretty place. "I could use some exercise after all this food."

"It looks like it might take an hour or more to bike there," Ryan informs me as he folds the map and slips it into his pocket. "You up for that?"

"Sure," I tell him. "After sitting for most of the day yesterday, it'll feel good to move around and get the lead out."

"Speaking of lead, want to get some coffee someplace else?" He lowers his voice. "The food here is great, but I think they could use some help with their java."

I nod. "Yeah, I agree. Let me get my backpack, and I'll be ready to go."

I jog up the three flights of stairs and notice that I'm slightly winded when I get to our room. I just hope I have what it takes to make this bike ride today.

I take a few seconds to brush my teeth and put on some lip gloss. Okay, not exactly primping, but I guess I sort of care what Ryan thinks of me. I'd attempt to do something with my hair, but with this damp air bringing out all the natural curl, it looks beyond help. Just in case it decides to get worse, I stick a scrunchy in my pack. If nothing else, I can always pull it back. Then I grab my sunglasses and stuff a hoodie into my pack, and I think I am ready to go.

We find this cute little coffeehouse called Cromwell's around the corner and order our coffees to go. Ryan gets a double latte, and I go for the mocha. We're barely out the door when we decide these are way better than what the B&B had to offer. Then we take our time as we stroll along, looking in the various shop windows and pausing to admire some contemporary art that's being featured in one of the galleries. The sun is shining, and the sky is perfectly clear as we casually make our way toward the bike-rental shop.

"Looks like a great day for a bike ride," Ryan comments as he drops his empty coffee cup into a dark-green garbage can that is actually rather classy looking.

"I totally love this place," I tell Ryan. We walk past a small grocery store that has its fresh produce artfully displayed outside the front door, neatly arranged in colorful rows, reminding me of a patchwork quilt in shades of reds and greens and purples. "I think I could live here."

"Wouldn't you miss your family?"

"Sure. But they could come visit me anytime they liked."

"It's a pretty long trip."

"Yeah, you're probably right." Even so, I do think I could live here.

Before long, we've got our bikes, and Ryan is pretty sure he knows which road to take. I don't admit that the idea of riding a bike on these narrow roads is freaking me out a bit. I'm actually wishing I'd taken the bike helmet that the rental guy told us was optional here. But the road we take doesn't appear to be very busy, and for the first half hour, we see only a couple of cars. We are going up and down rolling hills, and while the going down part is pretty fun, my thigh muscles are starting to burn from the uphill climbs. I'm barely keeping up with Ryan. After what I'm sure must be an hour of pretty vigorous riding, I spot what appears to be a mom-and-pop store, and I call out to Ryan that I need to stop and get something to drink.

"Sorry," he says when he comes back. "I didn't know you were getting so tired."

"I guess I'm not in very good shape." I wipe the back of my hand across my wet forehead. "I need to get some water."

"We don't have to be in such a hurry." He checks his watch. "Take your time and cool off. I'll stay with the bikes."

I attempt some long, deep breaths as I go into the tiny store. My legs are throbbing, and I feel pretty sure I won't ever be able to get back on that bike again. Maybe I should tell Ryan to go on without me.

"Cycling, are you?" asks an old man who's sitting on a stool behind an ancient cash register. "Good day for it too."

I see my blotchy red face in the mirror behind him and realize that I look like I'm about to have a heart attack or heatstroke. "Yes." I glance around the crowded shelves of the store. "Do you have any water?"

"Water?" He stands up and looks over his shoulder toward a door that I'm guessing must lead to the house behind the store. "You wish a drink o' water, do ya? Why, certainly. I'll be right back—"

"I mean *bottled* water," I say as I realize he's probably about to fetch me a glass of water from his house. "I want to buy a bottle of water."

"A *bottle* of water?" With a slightly befuddled expression, he scratches his head. "I canna understand why you Americans buy water in bottles when we have perfectly good drinking water coming right out of the spout. The wife tells me I should order this special water in the bottles for my shop, but I don't believe anyone in his right mind would really want to *buy* water." He nods to a tall cooler against the back wall. "Now, I do have what they call sports drinks, though. I've noticed that the one by the name of Lucozade is quite popular with sports enthusiasts."

I find the brand he's talking about. It resembles Gatorade, and I decide to buy a couple of bottles.

"You're a bit flushed," he says as he counts out my change. "Perhaps you should have a wee bit of a rest before you travel on."

I nod. "Yeah, I think you're right."

"Feel free to make yourself at home out there."

"Thank you."

Taking him at his word, I hand Ryan one of the drinks and flop down on the grass in front of the store and let out a loud groan.

"You okay?" Ryan leans over from where he's sitting on the bench and peers down at me with what appears to be bona fide concern.

"Maybe you should go on without me," I tell him as I slowly sit up and take a long swig of the red drink. "I didn't realize that I'm in such bad shape."

"I was probably riding too fast," he says apologetically. "We can slow it down. I think it's only about five more miles to the ferry, and we have plenty of time."

I really want to tell him to forget it, that I'm finished with biking and will be calling a cab to come pick me up, but his face looks so hopeful that I just nod and take another long drink. After a few minutes, I actually start to feel human again, and I force my tired body back onto the bike.

"You gonna be okay?"

I nod without speaking.

And so he takes off, but I notice that he goes a lot slower. Before long, I feel like I might be able to make it after all. He glances back at me from time to time, probably expecting to see me lying on the side of the road like a beached whale. But somehow I manage to keep up, and finally what looks like a seaport comes into sight.

We park and lock our bikes outside of the ferry ticket office and go inside to get our tickets, where the man informs us that it'll be an hour or so. "She's arunning late today," he says. "Maybe you'd like to get yourselves a pint at the pub next door. They've got a snooker table."

"Snooker table?" I quietly repeat to Ryan as we leave and head toward the pub. I can't imagine what that must be, but I'm thinking it's probably fairly disrespectful, and, consequently, I'm not even sure I want to go inside.

"Pool," he says as he opens the door.

"Pool?" I'm still not clear. Does he want to go swimming?

"Billiards," he says as if I'm mentally impaired.

"Oh, yeah." I nod as if I really did know this. Duh.

"Do you play?" he asks as he goes over to the pool table.

"As a matter of fact, not very well." I pick up a cue and pretend to study it for straightness.

"Want a drink?" he asks as he heads for the bar.

"Sure. Something lemony."

When he returns, he has a lemon drink for me and what appears to be a Guinness for himself. I frown at him.

"Does it bother you that I'm having a beer?"

I just shrug.

"I won't drink it if it really bugs you, Maddie. I just thought it sounded good after that ride."

I shrug again. "Do as you like."

He racks up the balls, and we begin to play pool, but I have to admit it does bug me that he's having a beer. I mean, it's barely noon. What's up with that?

We're about midway through the game, and fairly evenly matched, when Ryan asks me why I'm so quiet.

"I don't know." I lean over and take my shot at the nine ball, blowing it by several inches, probably due to the distraction of his question.

"It really does bug you that I'm having a beer, doesn't it?" he says, holding up his half-full glass.

"Maybe."

He walks over to the bar, sets the beer down, then orders the same lemon drink I'm having, and comes back. "Better?"

I kind of smile. "Maybe."

We continue playing pool, or snooker as the Irish call it, and just as Ryan is about to put in the eight ball, we hear a loud toot that we figure must be the ferry's horn. He misses his shot, but I concede the game to him since I still have two balls left on the table.

"I'm curious why you're so bugged about the beer thing," he says as we pick up our bikes. Our plan is to take them on the ferry and use them to tour the island. "Someone in your family have a drinking problem?"

I shake my head. "Just the opposite," I say. "My family is pretty conservative about alcohol." I consider the next statement I'm about to make and figure why not just get it out into the open. "And I'm a Christian." Even as I make this announcement, I feel kind of hypocritical.

He shrugs. "So?"

"Well, I just don't think Christians should drink."

"*All* Christians? You're making that decision for *all* Christians?"

Okay, I'm not quite sure how to respond to that.

"I'm curious as to how you reached this conclusion," he says as we wheel our bikes onto the pier. "I mean, that Christians aren't allowed to drink."

"It just seems pretty obvious."

"And how do you explain the fact that people in the Bible drank wine and that Jesus and his disciples drank wine? In fact, Jesus's first miracle was actually changing water to wine. How do you account for that?"

I'm surprised he knows anything about the Bible, having assumed he is *not* a Christian. "I don't think it was real wine," I say. "I've heard it was more like grape juice."

He kind of laughs but not in a mean way. "Right." Even so, it does make me feel uncomfortable, and I'm relieved I can focus my attention on wheeling the bike up the ramp that leads to the boat. Hopefully we can talk about something else. We park our bikes in the bike rack, and I start walking toward a door that looks like it leads to an inside seating area.

"Want to go up to the bow with me?" Ryan asks.

"Is it okay?"

"I don't know why not."

So I follow him along a walkway and down some stairs, then onto an open deck. Soon we are at the very front of the boat, standing in this little triangle where the bow leans out like a platform, extending right over the ocean. "Cool view," I say as I look down at the dark blue water below us.

"Yeah. I think this is the best seat in the boat. Except you have to stand."

Soon we are moving, and I have to agree with Ryan—this is the best seat in the boat! It feels kind of like flying as the bow moves up and down with the waves. "This is so cool," I say as I hold on to the railing and peer out.

"Look!" He's pointing at the water directly below us now and off to our right. "There's a dolphin!"

Sure enough, I see the dark gray shadow of a large fish swimming right along with the boat, keeping a perfect pace. And then I spot another just behind him. "Look, there are two!" Before long we have sighted about six of them, all racing alongside the boat as if this is a fun game they're used to playing.

"This is so awesome!" I say as I watch these graceful creatures moving along, occasionally jumping out of the water as if they're having a blast.

He nods with a huge smile. "I wish we could swim with them."

"It'd probably be cold down there."

"Maybe with a wetsuit."

The dolphins stick with us until we get closer to the island, and then they just sort of slip away. I'm disappointed to see them go. "That was so cool," I tell Ryan. "I've never seen a real dolphin before."

"Not even at SeaWorld?"

"I've never been there."

He looks at me like I have a cucumber for a nose. "Man, I guess Sid wasn't kidding."

"Kidding?"

"You really don't get off the farm much!"

As much as I want to punch him, I realize he's right. But, hey, I am here in western Ireland now, and we're about to see one of the most remote places in Connemara! And I actually managed to ride a bike all the way from Clifden. This is a really, really good day!

Six

As the boat draws closer to land, Ryan pulls out the brochure about Inishbofin and points toward what looks like a small castle. It almost appears to be part of a rock that's not too far away from the actual island.

"According to this," he reads, "that's a Cromwellian fort, which was used as a prison camp for Catholic priests."

"Why did they lock up the priests?" I ask as I stare at the dark rock fortress standing all by itself on a small stone island.

"Why?" Ryan repeats as if he's considering the answer himself. "I'm not sure anyone really knows why, Maddie. It's just the way they did things. The hatred between Catholics and Protestants pretty much defies common sense, don't you think?"

"Yeah. I know I don't get it."

Then he tells me how this island was picked by a dude named Coleman for the location of a monastery in 665. "Talk about a secluded place," he says. "It must've been totally uninhabited by anyone back then."

"What does Inishbofin mean?" I ask him since he's the one with the brochure and therefore the expert.

"It says here that *inish* is Irish for 'island' and that Inishbofin is the 'island of the white cows.'"

"I wonder how the cows got here," I muse as the boat pulls into the dock.

Soon we are wheeling our bikes down the ramp, and I can smell something cooking. It's well past noon, and I'm feeling pretty hungry. "Do you think there's any place to eat around here?"

"I don't know. The brochure says the population on the island is only about two hundred. That doesn't exactly sound like a bustling metropolis."

I remember the sweet little bakery across from our inn back in Clifden. They had a sign in the front window advertising sack lunches. I wonder if we should've bought a couple to bring with us.

But as it turns out, there are a couple of places to eat. They look pretty small and unimpressive. I suspect they're simply homes that double as pubs, but we place our orders from the very limited menus and are pleasantly surprised that, even out here in the sticks, the food's still good.

"I've heard that the Irish take their food very seriously," Ryan tells me as we finish our lunch of hearty sandwiches and chips. "It has to do with the potato famine and being starved out by the British. Maybe they're extra motivated to make sure they never get stuck with crummy food again."

"Works for me," I tell him.

Then we bike on the small roads that wind around the island, passing delightful little rock houses, small farms, lots of happy-looking white cows, and finally end up at the most amazing tide pools. We park our bikes and just walk and walk, examining the incredible sea life contained within these pockets of seawater while the tide is low.

"This is awesome," I say as I try to snap a picture of a purple crab and a bright orange sea anemone.

We take turns snapping photos of each other, I think to prove we were actually here. "This must be one of the most remote spots in Ireland," I say as we get onto our bikes and prepare to pedal back across the island.

"And isolated," says Ryan. "I read in the brochure that sometimes they are completely cut off from civilization during the winter, at times when it's too rough for the ferry to come out."

"Can you imagine?" I say as I gaze across the beautiful but rugged landscape along the edge of the sea. I continue thinking about how it would feel to live in a place like this as we ride down the narrow dirt road that twists and turns between the farms. I look at a small stone farmhouse, so vastly different from the two-story modern home I grew up in, and I try to imagine what it would really feel like to live in a place so far removed from the modern world. I'm not sure I could handle it.

We stop at a pub for drinks, and I'm relieved when Ryan gets a soda. Maybe he's gotten the whole Guinness thing out of his system now. I know I wouldn't complain about it if he has. We hear the sound of the ferry's horn and quickly finish our drinks and then hurry back to the boat.

"I'm so tired," I admit after we load our bikes and get our spot in the bow. "I hope I can make it back to town before dark."

"We could always call for a ride from the port," he says. "Maybe Sid could pick up you and the bike, and I could go ahead and just ride—"

"No," I say quickly, "I'll be fine. I guess I'll just be sleeping really, really well tonight."

To my relief, the return trip doesn't seem quite as long as the one this morning. That might be due to the cooler air or to the fact that I recognize the landmarks now, plus I keep telling myself it won't be long till we're back in town. We take a quick break at the little store, and this time a short, chubby woman (I suspect the wife) is working there, but I can tell she's ready to close up shop. I don't even bother to ask her about bottled water as I hurry to get our sports drinks. But after we're back outside, I call Sid to tell her we're running late.

"Don't worry," she says quickly. "I'm not done here yet. I can't believe the stuff I'm finding out. In fact, you guys might as well get yourselves some dinner if I'm not in Clifden by the time you're back."

I share this news with Ryan, and he frowns. "Man, I hope everything's going okay for her."

I kind of shrug. "Why shouldn't it be?"

His brow creases as he chucks his empty bottle into the trash can. "Ireland's kind of a weird place, Maddie. I mean, it's beautiful and amazing and mysterious and all that. But trust me, there's a lot of pain and heartache lying just beneath the surface. Seriously, I've grown up hearing these stories. It's not all as pretty as it appears."

I'm about to ask him what he means by this, but he's already getting back on his bike. So I take one last swig of my drink, toss my bottle into the trash, and despite the dull but growing ache in my hindquarters, I get back onto my bike as well. It takes my full concentration to just keep pedaling—left, right, left, right—but after a while I realize we're almost back to town. Just one more hill. I actually gasp out a desperate prayer as I'm creeping like a lethargic tortoise toward the top of the hill, begging God to strengthen my legs, which are actually shaking from fatigue right now. And when I reach the top, I beg him to help me make it down the decline without a serious crash and burn. Those rock walls bordering the road suddenly look formidable—not to mention I'm not wearing a helmet! *Dear God, just get me to the inn in one piece!*

And with some seriously sore muscles, I do make it. I feel a mixture of relief and exhaustion as we walk our bikes down the sidewalk toward the inn. And Ryan, very generously, offers to return the bikes for us. I don't even protest, nor do I experience a single pang of guilt as I watch him wheeling my detestable vehicle away. We agree to meet in the lobby downstairs around seven for dinner. Ryan has picked out the restaurant, and I am too ravenous to argue. It takes every last bit of my strength to make it up the three flights of stairs to my room. Haven't they heard of elevators in Ireland?

I strip off my stinky clothes, and to my surprise, the slow, drippy shower feels pretty fabulous. I let the hot water dribble down my worn-out body for nearly half an hour before I finally emerge and slowly get dressed again. I can't believe it's nearly seven already. And as hungry as I am, I'm a little worried about going back down all those stairs again—and then to think I have to come back up! Ireland is not for the faint of heart…or maybe that's the weary of body. At any rate, I should be in pretty good shape by the time I'm done with this vacation.

"No sign of Sid yet?" Ryan asks when I meet him in the lobby.

I shake my head. "I tried her cell phone, but it must be turned off. Anyway, I left her a message about where we'd be eating in case she gets here in time to meet us."

Okay, I haven't missed that this guy cleans up pretty well. You'd hardly know that he had been on an exhausting bike ride today. Whereas my cheeks are still flushed, and my legs feel like limp noodles. But, looking cool and rather attractive, Ryan has on a blue cotton sweater with the sleeves pushed up to his elbows. And it actually brings out the color of his eyes. Who knew they were so blue? I do feel a bit of relief that his khakis are wrinkled. I'm sure it's only from his suitcase, but I'm glad he doesn't look too perfect.

"Ready to go then?"

"I'm starving," I tell him.

"Me too," he says, and together we head for the door, which he politely opens for me. And, okay, I know this is nuts, but this feels almost like a date. "That was a good workout today, and you did a great job of keeping up, Maddie."

"Seriously?" I glance at him skeptically. "You really think so?"

"Yeah. You're in good shape."

"Thanks." I smile to myself as he points us toward the waterfront. He thinks I'm in good shape. Cool. "So how'd you hear about this restaurant anyway?" I ask as we stop at a corner and wait for a fish truck to pass. "Are you sure it's good?"

"The owner of the inn told me about it this morning. And when I turned the bikes in, the girl at the bike shop even mentioned it. She said the chef is a friend of hers and that he trained in Paris. Plus she told me they're having live music tonight."

"Cool," I say. But even though I say this, I immediately flash back to the live music we heard last night, remembering how stressed I got over the whole drinking thing. "Is this in a pub too?" I try to keep the suspicious tone out of my voice, but I think it's futile.

"Yep. It's a pub, Maddie." He gives me a sideways glance I can't quite read. "And you're going to have to get over your 'pubphobia.' I mean, this *is* Ireland. Pubs are just part of the culture here."

I force a stiff smile and try to act like I'm okay with this. "Yeah, I know." But as we turn the corner and go down a side street, I ask myself why I'm so irritated by this. Why is it so unsettling for me to be with someone who's consuming alcohol? It's not like I'm drinking. Even so, I want to ask Ryan if he plans to drink tonight. At the same time, I know I have no right to tell him what he can or cannot do. I mean, even my aunt thinks it's okay. He's probably right. I do need to get over this.

But as we enter the pub, it occurs to me that maybe I can say something to make Ryan understand where I'm coming from and why this is making me so uncomfortable. And then, out of the blue, I remember a quote from our youth pastor. He likes to say that "adversity can be opportunity in disguise." And it occurs to me that I might be able to use this "opportunity" for something good. I'm thinking maybe this is my big chance to actually share my faith tonight.

Okay, on second thought, I suppose that's kind of weird since my faith doesn't seem terribly strong right now. I mean, the truth is, I barely even pray anymore, and if I do, it's usually more of a desperate cry-for-help kind of prayer. So, really, who am I to witness to anyone?

Even so, I decide to jump right in. And it's not a coincidence that I broach the subject of religion right after Ryan orders himself a Guinness. Why not just get to the point?

"I know I already told you I'm a Christian," I begin kind of tentatively. "And although I'm not perfect, I do take my religion seriously." Okay, maybe that's a stretch. I *used* to take it seriously, but lately, well, I'm not even sure what I think. But he doesn't have to know everything about me.

"And?" He looks as if he expects me to continue, like I was really going somewhere with this. Like where?

"And…" I try to form a sensible thought in my head. "Well, I'm just not sure it's right for me to be hanging out in a beer-drinking establishment and with someone who would be underage back home but who thinks it's perfectly fine to drink over here in Ireland." Okay, I said it. It's out there. And now I sort of feel like my foot's in my mouth.

He slowly nods as if he's absorbing this. It actually gives me hope, and I start to think that maybe my witnessing idea is going to work after all.

"You see," I continue. "I think God has a lot more to offer us than the world does." I feel some enthusiasm in my voice now, as if maybe I've actually stumbled into something good. "And I think that he calls me, as a Christian, to be different from the world; he calls me to stand up for what I believe. Do you get that?"

He nods again.

"And so that's what I'm trying to do, Ryan. I realize I can't really judge you, but I need to remain firm and steadfast in my own faith and convictions."

"So what are you actually saying? I mean, in practical terms?"

I think about this, and I'm not really sure. I guess it feels like I'm taking some kind of a stand, but what kind of stand is it? What do I *really* mean? Should I stand up and leave this pub? Shake the dust off my feet and see if I can find someplace else (someplace that's not a pub) to eat in this town? Although that seems rather unlikely at this hour. I know the bakery serves sandwiches, but I don't think they're open at night.

"I totally accept that you're a Christian, Maddie," he says in a somewhat serious voice. "Really, I respect that completely. I also respect your conviction not to drink. But does that mean I shouldn't drink either?" Now he gets a thoughtful expression, as if something new has just occurred to him. "I mean, I don't want to be a stumbling block to you."

"A *stumbling block*?" Now, this is a familiar term—something

I've heard in church, and I think it's even in the Bible, although I'm not totally sure where. But I'm surprised that Ryan would use this kind of terminology. Where would he have heard it?

"Yeah," he continues. "I really wouldn't want my having a Guinness to tempt you to do something that God has clearly told you not to do. It just wouldn't be worth it for me. But at the same time, I don't think it's wrong for me to have a beer. Not to get drunk, you know, but just to enjoy it."

"Yeah, sure, but you're not a Christian."

"I'm not?" His left brow lifts just slightly.

"Are you?"

With no expression, he just nods as the waitress sets my lemon soda before me and a pint of Guinness in front of him. "Yep," he says as she walks away, "I am a Christian." Then he holds up the pint as if to make a toast. "Any problem with that?"

Okay, I feel like someone just pulled a fast one on me. "No," I say quickly. "I mean, if it's true." I frown at him. "You really *are* a Christian?"

He takes a swig, then sets his pint down. "Yep. I really am."

"And you think God's okay with you drinking?"

"I think God's fine with an occasional beer. I bet he'd have one himself if he were here with us."

I scowl at him.

"Seriously," he says. "I don't feel any guilt about it. Sure, I wouldn't want to get wasted. That would be stupid. And wrong. But a beer or two?" He shrugs. "No problem."

I shake my head. "I don't agree."

He holds up his pint again. "Then here's to disagreeing but still being friends."

I meekly hold up my soda as if I'm making this toast as well. But what I'm actually thinking is that this guy is all wet. He is totally wrong about this. And I'm not even sure he's a real Christian either. And by the time our food arrives, I've started to argue with him, trying to convince him that it's sinful to drink—especially sinful when you're a Christian. Although the more I think about it, the less I believe his claim about that.

"Hi, kids," says my aunt as the waiter shows her to our table.

"You made it," says Ryan, actually getting up to pull out the chair for her. Okay, he may be a failure as a Christian, but at least the boy has some manners.

"Yes," she says with excitement. "You wouldn't believe how this day has gone." She takes the menu from the waiter and quickly scans it. "I'll have the salmon," she tells him. Then glancing over to Ryan's nearly finished beer, she adds, "And a Guinness."

"And so you don't have to drink alone," says Ryan, "I'll have another."

She smiles at him. "Thank you. Hopefully that's only your first."

He nods, then glances over at me. "Maddie thinks Christians shouldn't drink."

"Oh." Sid considers this. "Well, I guess that's something between you and God…right, Maddie?"

I kind of nod, and then she launches into her story. "You guys aren't going to believe this," she says, "It was so weird. I drove out into the country just as I'd planned. It turned out to be this sweet little farm with sheep and chickens and even a milk cow. I was thinking this guy, Sean Potter, must be doing okay."

"He was one of the peace-camp kids?" Ryan asks.

"He was about six then. He's in his midthirties now. But I couldn't believe what happened." She lowers her voice, although I don't know how anyone would hear her in this noisy place. "Sean's wife told me to wait in the kitchen until he got off the phone. Then she took off to drive her daughter to school. So there I was, just sitting by myself in this sweet little Irish kitchen, and I couldn't help but hear Sean talking."

"And?" Ryan looks totally mesmerized by a story that actually sounds kind of boring to me. But then I'm still a little stuck on this whole Christians-drinking dilemma.

"And it sounded like Sean was making some kind of diabolic plan." Her eyes grow wide as she leans forward like she's going to say something very confidential. "I think he's actually part of the underground IRA."

"Seriously?" I blink at her. Is my aunt imagining things?

She nods with a somber expression. "*Very seriously.* And to make matters worse, it sounds like he's planning some kind of an attack in Belfast. I think it has to do with the Orange Rose on Beach Road."

"What's that?" I ask.

"A well-known Protestant pub."

I kind of shrug. Like I would really care if someone bombed a pub. Okay, I take that back; I guess I probably would.

"You overheard *that*?" Ryan looks stunned.

"Well, I couldn't catch everything." She glances over her shoulder as if she's really worried that someone could be listening. "But I heard enough to make me suspicious."

"Did this guy, this Sean person, have any idea you could hear him?" asks Ryan.

"I slipped outside just as he hung up the phone. I pretended to be interested in the herb garden, which was really quite nice."

"And then you went ahead and did the interview anyway?" I ask, thinking I probably would've concocted some excuse to get away from this crazy guy.

"Yes." She nods with sad eyes. "There's a story here. How could I let it get away?"

"Did he mention anything about the underground IRA in your interview?" asks Ryan.

"No. And I even asked about it. But he said those recent stories had been blown out of proportion, and he acted as if he were still very interested in peace. He said that's why he left Belfast, to get away from the violence. In fact, he did such a great job of talking it up that I was almost convinced."

"But not quite?"

She sighs. "I know what I heard. Sean is just one of those Irishmen with the gift of the blarney."

"So what are you going to do about it?" I ask. "Shouldn't you warn someone?"

"I already did."

"Who did you tell?" asks Ryan with a worried expression.

"My editor back at the magazine. I figured that would be the safest route. He'll contact the authorities from over there. We don't want anyone over here tracking this back to us."

He nods with very serious eyes.

"Are we in danger?" I ask.

Sid pats my hand. "No, sweetie. We're not in any real danger. But it was pretty exciting getting the inside story…and sad…"

"Do you think you really stopped something?" I ask.

She shrugs and takes a sip of her Guinness. "I sure hope so."

"Time will tell," says Ryan.

"But you can see how this puts a whole new twist on my story." She stares off into space. I almost think I can see the wheels spinning in her head. "It's not what I hoped for, but just the same I can't wait to start writing. People need to know what's going on here. Disappointing as it is, it will do no good to hide these facts."

"You won't put yourself in danger, will you?" says Ryan with real concern. "I mean, you know what kinds of things can happen over here."

"Don't worry, Ryan. I'll be very careful. Especially since I have you two with me. In fact, I may have to act more like a tourist than a reporter now."

"For a cover?" I say.

"Yes. I'll continue with my peace-camp interviews, but I'll make it all seem fairly low-key, like we're mostly here just to see the sights."

"Why?" I ask. "Do you think someone is actually watching you?"

"Not yet."

"This is too weird," I say.

"Don't be worried, Maddie," she says in a comforting tone. "I'm sure I'm making this into far more than what it really is. And I suppose I could be totally wrong about Sean too." She glances over her shoulder again. "Just the same, you guys are sworn to secrecy about this. Understand?"

"Of course." Ryan gives her a firm nod.

"Sure," I say in a light tone. "Like who would I tell anyway?"

She gives me a fairly stern look, as if this really isn't funny. *"No one."*

Okay, that sort of worries me. What have I gotten myself into?

Seven

For the next couple of days, we act like regular tourists, tooling around Galway County and touring castles, monasteries, formal gardens, seaports, the highlands, and even a small, family-owned farm. (I promised my dad I'd check out the agriculture.) One of my favorite spots was a castle that I actually discovered myself while taking an early morning walk. The castle is actually more of a ruins but really mysterious looking. It's off of a gravel road that's just a little ways out of Clifden, and I had to walk through a field inhabited by some rather intimidating bulls. But being a farm girl, I just kept my cool as well as a wary eye on the animals until I climbed over the fence stile. There before me, shrouded in fog, stood a big stone structure that looked like something right out of a fairy tale. I almost expected to see a captive princess waving from one of the high arched windows. But as I got closer, I saw that it was only a shell of a castle. All windows and doors were missing, and there was grass, vines, and even some small trees growing inside. Still, it was fun to explore the grounds, and I considered the people who dwelled there in previous centuries. I can't imagine that the castle had ever been very warm or cozy in Ireland's cool and damp climate, not to mention that it was located quite close to the sea. I guess I don't envy whoever once lived there.

On Friday we check out of our inn and head north toward Donegal County, driving all day through miles and miles of beautiful, lush green countryside. It's around five o'clock when my aunt finally parks the car in a small seaport town called Malin.

"Are we in Northern Ireland?" I ask as I climb out of the backseat and pause on the sidewalk to have a good stretch. From what I can see, this place doesn't look much different from Galway. The weather has turned cold and windy, so I immediately reach for my thick wool sweater. It's hard to believe it's nearly July.

"Not officially," my aunt tells me as she opens the trunk. "But we're really close. At least as the crow flies."

"So what made you want to come here?" I ask. "Not that it doesn't look interesting."

"Malin Head is where Ryan's ancestors lived. I thought he'd enjoy seeing it. Check out his roots, if he likes."

"Why did they leave?" I ask Ryan. "Was it due to the potato famine?"

"No. That didn't have too much of an impact on my family. Plus they left quite a bit later." He pauses from helping my aunt unload the bags. "My grandparents immigrated to the States a few years before World War II started. My grandpa's folks had been fishermen for generations, but he and my grandma were looking for a better life. My dad was the first one of their kids to be born in the U.S."

"Oh." I sling my backpack over one arm and reach for my

wheelie bag. I want to ask Ryan how his dad died but can't think of the right way to put it just now. And maybe it's none of my business anyway. "So, are your grandparents still around?"

He closes the trunk with a thud. "Just my grandma, but she lives in a nursing home in Tacoma, and I think she might have Alzheimer's or something. She doesn't really know anyone anymore."

Another wave of compassion washes over me. Ryan seems so cut off from his family. It's like he's totally on his own. I can't imagine what that would be like. And it makes me feel bad to think of some of the things I've said to him these past few days, not to mention the way I've treated him in regard to drinking his occasional Guinness. Why am I so petty?

We check into our hotel, and since the rooms are pretty small, Sid decides we'll each have a room of our own. "That way I can work on my article without disturbing you," she tells me as she hands me a brass key.

"Works for me," I tell her. Trust me, I'm not complaining about having my own room. I mean, my aunt is nice and everything, but I'm just not used to sharing a room with anyone. A break will be nice.

"Shall we meet in the lobby in about an hour or so?" she asks as we part ways in the hallway. "I've got some phone calls to make."

"Sounds great," Ryan says as he unlocks the door directly across from mine. "I might take a little walk to check this place out. Maybe I'll run into some long-lost relative." He laughs. "Want to join me, Maddie?"

"Sure," I tell him as I fumble for my room key. "If you want company, that is."

"Can you be ready in a few minutes?" he asks.

"No problem."

I quickly toss my bags onto my bed, freshen up a little, pull on my fisherman's-knit sweater, then hurry back out to join him.

The wind is really starting to whip as we leave the hotel. "Looks like it's going to rain," I say, speaking loudly to be heard over the wind.

"You up for this?" he yells back.

"Sure," I say. "It's kinda fun."

He points across the road. "Want to check out the bay?"

I nod and pull the collar of my sweater up around my neck, and we hurry in that direction, straight into the wind. And even though it's biting cold, it's also invigorating. We walk for several minutes, but Ryan seems to know where he's going. And after a while we find ourselves down by the docks, just in time to see fishermen hurrying to unload crates and tie things down, as if they're getting ready for a storm. Everyone seems busy, and we try not to get in their way as we look at the various fishing boats. Then it starts to rain. Not just small drops either. It's like the sky has literally opened up, and the rain is coming down by the bucketfuls.

"Let's get out of this," says Ryan as he grabs me by the arm and practically drags me through a dark doorway right off the street. My eyes adjust to the dim light, and I instantly recognize that we're in a pub. It figures. But at least it's warm and dry, and I notice there's even a fire crackling in a small stone fireplace over in the corner. If it weren't a pub, it would be very inviting.

Ryan leads me over to a tall table situated right in front of the window, and I sit down and peel off my damp sweater. "This is nice," I say as I peer out the cloudy glass to see the docks and boats being pelted by the rain.

"Really?" One of his brows lifts in a skeptical expression.

"Yeah. Really."

"So are you going to wig out if I order a Guinness?"

I consider this. "No," I finally say, "I am not."

"Cool. I don't want one, but I appreciate the flexibility." He smiles, and it occurs to me that he has a very nice smile.

I'm not sure why, but for the first time since we've been in Ireland, I don't feel all that concerned that I'm sitting in a pub or that Ryan might have a beer. It seems like no big deal. Whether this means I've made some kind of spiritual compromise is a mystery to me. But at the moment, I don't care. I'm just glad to be in a dry place.

We order our drinks. Coffee for Ryan and hot tea for me. "So how does it feel to be in the same region where your father's family came from?" I glance around the sparsely populated pub. "Think anyone here is related to you?"

He studies the guys sitting at the bar. They look like fishermen, but I don't see any resemblance to Ryan. "Who knows?"

"Want me to ask if anyone here knows someone by the name of McIntire?" I say in a slightly teasing tone.

He laughs. "I'm not sure I'm ready for that just yet. I feel like I need to get my bearings first. You know?"

I nod. "Yeah, it must seem kind of strange."

"Yeah. It's really making me think about my dad. To be honest, I haven't done that much. I mean, I never really knew him. And my mom didn't speak of him much. At least not until this past year."

"What was he like?"

"Well, like I said, he was born in America, but according to my mom, his heart belonged to Ireland."

"How's that?"

"I suppose it was a result of hearing family stories and stuff. But during the seventies, he really got caught up in Northern Ireland politics. He wanted to come over here, but his parents said he had to finish college first. So after he graduated, he came. I guess it was supposed to be just for a visit, but then he decided to stay."

"For good?"

"For good or for bad."

"Huh?"

"I think he was kind of torn. I mean, he really loved my mom, and he knew she didn't want to live here, not back then when things were such a mess. And then she got pregnant with me, so they went back to America." He sighs.

"But then he returned to Ireland?"

"Like I said, he came back when I was a baby. It was supposed to be a short trip…"

"But he never came home again."

"Yep." Then he takes a drink of his coffee.

"Because he died here," I offer, feeling as if I'm the one telling Ryan's story.

"Yep."

"How did he die, Ryan? Do you know?"

"My dad was a member of the IRA."

"Really?" I blink in surprise. All I know about the IRA is that they want to reunite Ireland through means of violence. They're the ones who were responsible for the bombings and shootings when Sid and Danielle came here. And even though they've "disarmed," it seems their influence is still around—especially after hearing about Sid's interview with the dude who's plotting to bomb a Belfast pub. That pretty much creeps me out.

"Yeah. My dad was really sympathetic to the IRA cause. Like lots of other Irishmen, he resented the British and wanted them out of Ireland completely. Like I said, he grew up hearing his parents' stories. He knew all about the kinds of persecutions that had gone on here for centuries. My ancestors lost valuable land to the British, and even though my grandparents pretty much recovered from poverty not long after they immigrated to the U.S., I don't think they ever got over the painful memories."

I nod as I refill my teacup.

"So, anyway, my dad met my mom at a party in Belfast, and according to my mom and Sid, he fell head over heels for her." Ryan kind of smiles. "After meeting my mom, my dad somehow tracked her back to the peace camp, and he started writing her letters with poems, and he sent her flowers and all kinds of things.

The poor guy was totally smitten. I guess he even volunteered to help out at the camp, which seems kind of weird, considering he was a member of the IRA. But he just wanted to be near her."

"He was really in love."

"Well, my mom was a pretty cool lady."

I nod. "Yeah. That's what Sid always said too."

"Anyway, she finally agreed to date him, and by the end of the summer, they were engaged. He even talked my mom into staying over here longer, and your aunt went home alone."

"I didn't know that."

"I don't think Sid was too happy about it."

"Didn't she like your dad?"

"She didn't trust him."

"Oh."

"And, of course, she wasn't exactly happy about something else…"

"The broken-heart thing?"

"Yeah, Ian was a good friend of my dad's."

"Seriously?"

"Yeah. That's how they met."

"Was Ian an IRA member too?"

Ryan shrugs. "I don't know for sure."

"But he might've been."

He shrugs. "Anyway, my parents got married, and they stayed in Ireland for several years. And suddenly it was time to go."

"You mean because your mom was pregnant?"

"There was another reason."

"What?"

Ryan looks at me as if he's trying to decide how much to tell me. I really want him to trust me, but I don't want to push him. "My dad was in over his head," he finally said. "He either had to leave the country or risk going to prison."

"Oh." I'm still trying to process the fact that Ryan's very own father was really in the IRA, trying to grasp how his dad did something that could've landed him in prison. Was it murder? bombings? What?

"Anyway, it was a good time for them to get out. I know my mom was relieved."

"So did your mom know about his IRA connection?"

"Not before they were married. But she found out later."

"Man, that must've been tough. I mean, here she is, working in the peace camps, trying to bring unity, and your dad is out there…" I don't finish the sentence. I know it would sound terrible to say what I'm really thinking. *Was Ryan's dad a murderer?*

"It was hard, but she really did love him. And I think she understood what he was doing—at least on some levels. Just the same, she didn't agree with the IRA or violence. The truth is, she only started to talk to me about this stuff when she knew she was dying. I guess she didn't want to leave without answering some of my questions."

"I can understand that."

"Unfortunately, I still have lots of questions."

"So what made your dad come back here? Do you know?"

"Sort of. My parents settled in Seattle, not far from my dad's parents. My mom didn't know it, but my dad never gave up his IRA connections or the cause. He came back here to make a delivery."

"A delivery?"

"Money."

"Money?"

"Yeah. There were a lot of Irish sympathizers in my grandparents' circle of friends. When they heard how bad things were getting over here, they started collecting funds to help the IRA."

"And your father smuggled the money over here?"

"That's what my mom told me. And I guess it was successful. He'd called my mom shortly after the delivery. He told her that he was about to leave for the Belfast airport. But he never got there. Someone put a bomb in the car."

"Oh no."

He nods sadly. "But that's not all."

"What?"

"Ian McMahan was the one driving my dad to the airport."

"So Ian McMahan was killed too?"

Ryan barely nods. "Pretty sad stuff, huh?"

I just shake my head. "Wow. That is really depressing…and tragic."

"I guess that's what really caused Sid and my mom to bond for life. I mean, they'd always been friends, but it's like they became sisters or something. Sid was like part of our family then. Although I do have some other aunts and uncles, on my dad's side, they're all a lot older than my mom, and she never encouraged me to get to know them. I think she was afraid I'd get caught up in their politics too. Anyway, Sid's been more of an aunt to me than any of them."

"Wow. That's quite a story."

"I figured it was about time to tell you."

I look into his eyes and am surprised at how much I'm starting to respect this guy. It's like there's so much more to him than I ever imagined. And even though the whole IRA thing with his dad makes me uncomfortable, I'm glad he's opened up like this. "Thanks for telling me."

"I asked Sid if it was okay to tell you—I mean, the part about her and Ian."

"She didn't mind?"

"No, she thought you should know."

I sigh. "Wow, I'm still trying to take it all in."

"I know. It's a lot to digest." He points to his watch. "Speaking of digest, if we're going to meet Sid for dinner, we'd better get back."

We're barely out the door when we are hit with a gust of wind and stinging raindrops that seem to be falling parallel to the ground.

"Want to run?" Ryan asks.

"Sure," I say. And to my surprise, he grabs my hand, and the two of us start to run down the street, forging our way through what is starting to feel like quite a storm. But I must admit that I like the secure feel of his hand tightly gripping mine. Okay, I remind myself, it's only to get us to the hotel more quickly. And it is handy having his help as we leap across mud puddles and make a mad dash for several blocks. It's no reason for me to start getting all starry-eyed. After all, Ryan and I are just friends. Nothing more.

"Thanks," I tell him once we're safely inside the lobby.

"No problem." He removes his parka and gives it a little shake.

I look down at my rather soggy sweater and realize it's probably not going to shake out quite so nicely. "I better go find something dry to put on before it's time for dinner."

As I head to my room, all I can think about is the warm feeling of Ryan's hand wrapped around mine—and how much I liked it!

Eight

"Y ou look like a drowned rat," says Sid as we meet in the hallway.

"It's raining like crazy out there," I tell her. "And the wind is going nuts. Do they have hurricanes in Ireland?"

She laughs. "I don't think so. But they can have some pretty wild storms, especially on the coastline. Maybe we should stay in tonight. We could eat in the hotel restaurant instead of going out."

"Fine with me." I unlock my door. "I just came up to dry off a little. Ryan is already downstairs."

We agree to meet in the restaurant, and I frantically dig through my bags searching for the perfect thing to wear. I even try on several things, tossing the rejects onto a pile that's growing on my bed. Finally I decide on a cappuccino brown V neck that I think looks kind of sophisticated on me. Okay, at the same time I'm asking myself why go to this much trouble? Like who really cares how I look?

But the truth is, I care, and I know it's because of Ryan. Then I spend too much time trying to tame my hair, which is totally hopeless after the wind and rain. I try pulling it back in a scrunchy, but that only makes me look like a poof head. Finally I give up and just let it hang wild around my shoulders. Then I put on some mascara, some lip gloss, a bit of blush, and even a pair of earrings Sid got for me when we stopped for lunch in Donegal today. She thought the green stones were about the same color as my eyes. Okay, I don't look too bad.

I find my aunt and Ryan already seated at one of the few tables in this tiny restaurant. They're both looking at a newspaper, but my aunt seems upset. Her face is pale, and I think I see tears in her eyes.

"What's wrong?" I ask as I sit down.

Ryan holds up the newspaper for me to see. It's the front page, and the headline says, "Bomb in Belfast Pub Kills 2, Injures 17."

"Oh no."

"I feel so responsible," says Sid.

"But you warned them."

She nods, pulling a tissue from her purse. "And John assured me that they were on it, that nothing would happen." She glances at her watch. "Let's see… It's still morning there. I think I'll call him." She reaches for her cell phone, then excuses herself, taking the newspaper with her.

"That's so sad," I say as I watch her leave.

The waiter is approaching our table now. "Is anything wrong?" he asks with concern.

"No," I say quickly. "My aunt just needs to make a phone call. We'll order when she comes back."

He nods and offers to get us something to drink, but we both decide to wait for Sid.

"I wonder if it really was the guy she interviewed," Ryan says once the waiter is out of earshot.

"If it wasn't, it's a pretty ironic coincidence."

"I can't believe he would be so careless, having that conversation when she was right there."

"Well, it was really his wife who was careless," I remind him. "Remember she was the one who told Sid to wait in the kitchen."

His eyes widened. "Do you think that woman actually wanted her husband to get caught?"

"Maybe she just wanted to prevent what she knew would turn into a serious tragedy."

"Or maybe she didn't know about any of it."

"It all seems so senseless." I pick up the menu and try to focus on the words. "I mean, killing people you don't even know? And for what? Just to make a point? For vengeance? I really don't get it."

He shakes his head. "It goes deep, Maddie. Generations and generations of hatred and fighting, lying and cheating. It might not make sense to us, but it probably does to some people."

"Like your dad?"

He frowns, and I feel bad. I wasn't trying to say his dad was evil, but I know it must have sounded that way.

"I know my dad made some mistakes," he says slowly. "But now that I'm here in Ireland…I don't know… It's like I can almost understand."

"You can understand the IRA?"

"In a way. I mean, they weren't all violent. And their goal was to reunite Ireland. But violence often got in the way. And now we have the RIRA."

"What's the RIRA?"

"I was just reading that article about the bombing in Belfast, and they mentioned the RIRA. The extra *R* stands for *real,* as in the Real Irish Republican Army. Anyway, that's what this new generation of IRA members call themselves, and they're taking credit for today's bombing."

"Not the old IRA?"

"No. The new RIRA refuses to disarm and refuses to give up this fight."

"How can you be sure that the new RIRA isn't really just another name for the old IRA?"

"Because the old IRA had more dignity."

"How do you know that?"

"I've done some reading. I did a little research before we came here. I wanted to know why my dad had been pulled into this. And I could partly understand it."

"Meaning you sympathize with them?"

"Of course. So did you when we first got here. I remember you saying that you thought Ireland should just reunite."

"But not with bombs and guns."

"I agree. Not with bombs and guns. But, don't forget, the British army uses the same means to keep Ireland under their control. How do you fight back when someone is shooting at you?"

"This is way over my head," I admit. "I want to understand it, but the whole IRA and RIRA thing kind of overwhelms me."

"I know," he says. "I feel like that too. And I hope you understand that in no way do I condone the RIRA. What they did today was totally wrong. But I guess I'm just starting to feel differently toward the original IRA, the ones who wanted to unite Ireland, to be free of British rule."

"But through means of force?"

"How do you think our country won its independence?"

"I know." I shake my head. "But that was so long ago."

"Think about the world in general, Maddie. How do countries get liberated? What about Iraq, Iran, Afghanistan?"

"I'm sorry, but I hate war."

"So do I. But maybe it's inevitable—sometimes."

I'm wishing Sid would come back. Maybe she could carry on this conversation with Ryan. It just seems to be irritating me.

"Anyway…I'm starting to see things differently. I'm starting to ask questions that I wouldn't have even considered before."

"Questions about your dad?"

He nods. "Yes. Like why he was pulled into their cause. Have I been missing something? I've done the research; I know that thousands of innocent Irish have died as a result of British inter-ference. But it wasn't as if I really cared. Then suddenly, being here in Malin, where my family's roots go back for centuries, and hear-ing about the bomb in Belfast—not to mention how this has impacted Sid—well, I guess I'm starting to feel sort of guilty. Like maybe this has something to do with me. And maybe it's time I come to grips with my own heritage and what it means to be Irish. Instead of sitting around just accepting things for what they seem. Maybe I need to open my eyes."

Okay, this is really messing with my mind. Is Ryan saying he has become sympathetic to the IRA? or even the RIRA? Because that just seems crazy to me. I'm about to point this out to him when Sid returns.

"Sorry to be gone so long," she says as she sits back down. Her eyes are still red, and I can tell she's still upset.

"Did you talk to your editor?" I ask. I'm so relieved to have her back. It gives me a break from this confusing conversation with Ryan. I wonder if she realizes how he's feeling. Like does he plan to run off and join the IRA or the RIRA or whatever it's called? Okay, I realize I'm being ridiculous.

"We had a nice long talk." She unfolds her linen napkin and places it in her lap, releasing a long sigh. I can't tell if it's from frustration or relief. Maybe both.

"And?" I prompt her.

"And John said he did inform the authorities, and he said he was quite specific about what I told him. He even gave the name and address of"—she glances around to make sure no one's listening, then lowers her voice—"of Sean Potter."

"Do you really think he's the one who did it?" I ask in a quiet tone.

"I definitely think he's part of it. But I doubt he actually did it himself. John did confirm that Sean is suspected of being a member of RIRA."

"How did he find that out?" asks Ryan.

"Friends in high places, I suspect." Then she smiles at the waiter who's approaching our table and changes the subject to the weather. We place our orders, but when the food comes, we aren't very hungry. Our waiter is concerned that something is wrong with the food.

"No," says Ryan, nodding to the newspaper still on the table. "It's just hearing the news in Belfast. I think it took our appetites away."

"It's a shame," says the waiter, "but a reminder as well."

"A reminder?" says Sid.

"That it's not over." His brow creases. "It'll never be over."

My aunt pays the bill, and we leave. I'm curious what the waiter meant by that. Does he sympathize with the British pub owner, or is he saying that the Irish people will never back down from wanting to rule themselves?

My aunt pauses in the lobby. She's looking at the small television that's nested in the bookcase. The news is on, and they're showing scenes of what must be the site of the bombing in Belfast. Naturally, this would be the hot topic of the day. We decide to sit down and watch. The news anchor is going through the expected details, telling the names of those killed and giving an update on the state of the injured parties. "Our sources confirm that the RIRA has already taken credit for the brutal attack." Then they begin showing photos of RIRA members and even listing their names. This is followed by footage of several members who have already been placed under arrest.

"There's Sean Potter," Sid whispers, pointing at a fair-haired man trying to hide his face as a policeman ushers him toward a brick building.

"Do you think he'll figure out who turned him in?" asks Ryan.

My aunt just shrugs.

Now the newscaster is talking about past RIRA attacks, comparing them to today's violence. "The most recent RIRA incidents have been limited to the greater London area," he says. "But today's bombing in Belfast has provided a heartbreaking reminder of the Omagh incident in 1998. Twenty-nine civilians were murdered on that day, primarily unsuspecting women and children out to enjoy a carefree holiday and to shop for school uniforms." More footage is shown now, and I am horrified at the scenes of rubble mixed with mangled bodies. "Hundreds more were injured that day. But many hoped that the tragedy in Omagh would bring an end to this era. The public outrage effected an RIRA cease-fire that eventually inactivated the group. And some claimed it was the end of terrorism in our country. Sadly, we now know that is not to be the case…"

"What a waste!" Sid stands up and shakes her fist at the TV. "What a sad and senseless waste. And to think that Danielle and I believed we were actually making a difference back then. We honestly thought the peace camps might change things. And then to come here and find out that—" And now she is crying. Both Ryan and I go to her. We wrap our arms around her and end up in a big group hug.

"It's going to be okay, Sid." Ryan pats her on the back.

"Yeah," I echo. "Something good is going to come out of this." Okay, I have no idea what that "something good" might be, but it sounds encouraging. We say a few more consoling things, and then, to my surprise, Ryan actually says a prayer. He asks God to use the three of us while we're in Ireland, and he asks for a special blessing on our trip and also for our safety. By the time he finishes, I discover I am crying too.

"Thanks, Ry." My aunt reaches for her tissue packet and shares one with me. We both dry our eyes. "I think we needed that prayer." She looks at me. "I know I did."

I nod as I wipe my nose. "Me too."

Ryan lets out a deep breath. "Well, I got to thinking that maybe God has a plan for this trip. Maybe it's supposed to be more than just a fun vacation."

Sid nods. "Yes. I'd like to believe that too. And tomorrow I have another appointment with a former peace-camp kid. It's a woman this time. Perhaps it'll go better. At the very least I'm hoping and praying she's not a member of the RIRA. Otherwise, I may just can this project completely and fly us all back home on Sunday."

"But what about your other story?" I ask her. "Didn't you want to write about the RIRA too?"

She sort of nods. "Yeah. But I can only take so much, Maddie. And it's possible to write that story from the safety of home. Trust me, I will not keep us here if I feel that we're in any real danger. I thought I'd gotten over it, but the truth is, I don't really trust Ireland."

Well, I'm hoping she's wrong. I've actually been enjoying Ireland, and I'm not ready to go home yet. Whether this is because I want to see more of this beautiful yet troubled Emerald Isle or is due to my developing interest in one particular traveling companion, who is full of surprises, I'm not completely sure. But I'd like to find out!

Nine

For some reason I wake up extra early the next morning, but when I get down to the lobby, I don't see Ryan or my aunt or anyone else for that matter. I wait a few minutes and consider calling their rooms, but I would hate to wake them if they're sleeping in, so I decide to venture out by myself. As I go out the door, I can hardly believe there'd been such a wild storm in Malin last night. The air is perfectly still now, and the sky is a brilliant blue. The sun, barely up, feels warm on my head, and the day promises to be beautiful. I look up and down the street, trying to decide which way to go. Finally I notice there seems to be more traffic heading south, so that's the way I go too.

There is something so cool about being on your own in a totally new place. Seriously, it makes me feel very grown-up and sophisticated. Okay, I'd never admit this to anyone, because it sounds pretty juvenile and brings to mind the whole "fresh off the farm thing," but this independence does make me feel older. It's like I'm out and about, walking down a street on the other side of the planet, and I can pretty much take care of myself. Or so I'd like to think.

As it turns out, I've walked the right direction, and before long I'm in the center of this quaint little town. Malin is a port town, similar to Clifden, but with a personality all its own. The shops are situated around this pretty parklike, grassy area, and everything is very clean and neat and immaculately groomed. It's so perfect that it could almost be a movie set. Even the air smells clean.

My first stop is a small bakery, where the aroma of something delicious is wafting onto the street. I go inside and order a coffee along with the breakfast special, which turns out to be a big fluffy croissant, an egg, and a thick slice of bacon. Then I find a small round table that's topped with shiny black marble and is situated by a window that faces the village green. I sit down happy. I take a bite of what I might describe as sort of an Irish-style Egg McMuffin but am pleased to say it's about a hundred times better.

It feels as though it's going to be a perfect day. I take my time eating, then get a refill on my coffee and purchase some raspberry scones, just out of the oven—one to eat if I like and a couple to take back to the sleepyheads. Life just doesn't get any better than this. That's when I notice an Irish newspaper on the next table, and the sad headlines about the continued investigation of the bombing in Belfast hit me with a bolt of reality.

"Hey, Maddie." I look up to see Ryan coming toward me, waving with one hand and holding a cup of coffee in the other.

"What are you doing here?" I ask. Okay, dumb question.

"Looks like great minds think alike." He grins and points to the chair across from me. "That taken?"

"Help yourself."

"Why do you look so glum?"

I point at the newspaper. "I was actually feeling pretty great, and then I saw those headlines and got reminded of the bombing."

He looks at the front page and frowns. "Yeah. That's a real downer." He points to my little white bag of scones. "That your breakfast?"

So I explain to him what I had, and he goes and orders the same. Now I know this is a small thing, but it makes me feel important to actually give him a good tip for a change. Before long he is back, chowing down his breakfast special. Then I offer him a scone, and he's all over it. I'm just starting to eat mine when Sid comes in and joins us.

"Get the breakfast special," he tells her. "Maddie discovered it, and it's really good."

Finally we've finished our three stages of breakfast as well as the amazing berry scones, and Sid tells us she has to head over to Moville to interview the peace-camp woman.

"You going to be all right?" I ask. I think I can see dark shadows beneath her eyes, and I suspect she's still feeling bad about the Belfast bombing. Not that she should.

She sighs. "Yeah. I just hope that Molly's life has turned out better than Sean's."

"Do you want us to come along?" I offer.

She shakes her head and stands up. "No. I need to do this alone." She glances at Ryan and me. "You guys going to be okay on your own today? I mean, in light of recent unsettling developments."

"I'm not a bit worried," I say.

"I'm fine," he tells her. "I'm even thinking about going fishing. The manager at the hotel gave me the name of a charter boat that goes out twice a day."

"Sounds good," she says as she heads for the door. "Have fun."

"Fishing?" I turn and look at Ryan like he's crazy.

"Yeah, it's in the blood, remember?"

"Oh yeah."

"You want to give it a try?"

I consider this. Okay, it is tempting, not because of the fishing part, but simply because I'd like to be around Ryan. Even so, the idea of baiting hooks and handling slimy, wiggly, smelly things is just not worth it. I've been fishing with my dad and brother enough times to know it's not really my cup of tea. "No thanks," I say.

"So what are you going to do then?" he asks.

"Just hang out in town, I guess."

He glances at his watch. "Well, if I'm going to be on the ten o'clock boat, I better get moving."

So we part ways, and I notice that shops are starting to open. I decide to check them out. It's ironic that I was enjoying being on my own earlier today, because now I feel just a little bit lonely. To my dismay, it doesn't take long to look at all the shops—at least the ones that appeal to me—and finally I find myself sitting on a bench in the village green, wishing I'd gone fishing with Ryan. I mean, I could've just enjoyed the boat ride and sat in the sun. No one could've forced me to actually fish. What was I thinking?

I consider returning to the hotel, but that seems kind of

pathetic. It's such a nice day, and here I am in Ireland! That's when I notice the bike-rental shop again. I already walked past it once, and it occurs to me that maybe I just need some wheels to get around. So I rent myself a bike, along with a helmet, and as I'm studying a tourist map of Malin Head and trying to figure out which way I should go, the girl behind the counter asks if I'm interested in going on a bike tour.

"When?"

"They usually leave at eleven or so, and they get back around six in the evening."

"Is it possible to join a group today?"

"Quin?" She yells to the back room, and a guy in his twenties emerges with a wrench in hand. "Are there any spots left in today's bike tour?"

"Aye, there's a spot, but that would make us an even dozen. We canna have more than that."

She looks at me. "Are you interested?"

"I'm not the greatest biker," I admit.

"Oh, I'm sure you'll be fine," she says. "It's not a strenuous ride, and some of the bikers are retired folks." She smiles. "And you look fit. Shall I sign you up then?"

"Sure." I nod. "Sounds good."

"It's twenty-five euro," she tells me, "but that includes a tasty lunch in Malin Head and a short ferry ride across the bay. It's really quite nice."

So I sign up for the tour, then head back to the hotel to put on shorts and pick up some things. By the time I make it back to the shop, there are several other bikers already gathered by the village green. And the bike-shop woman wasn't lying. Some of these people do look pretty old. I'm guessing I won't be in last place this time. Pretty soon we're all there and ready to go.

"I'm Quin McMahan," the man I met in the rental shop tells everyone. "I'll be your guide today. And my wife, Darby, will bring up the rear with the van." He points to a white van parked nearby, then holds up what looks like a shortwave radio like my dad uses with my brother when they go hunting. "We'll queue up along the road, giving plenty o' room between the cycles, and Darby and I will communicate with these handy-dandy devices to make sure all's well. If you have a problem during the ride, just wait by the side of the road, and Darby will stop by to pick you up before long. She knows a bit about bike mechanics and is even taking her nurse's certificate, so she can be useful if you have a health problem as well." He winks at his wife. "Naturally, we ensure that all who start on our bike trips make it safely back to town. Even if they come home via the van."

Some of the older folks are joking about this possibility, but Quin reassures them that the ride isn't difficult and that he won't be pushing it in the least. This is a relief to me. We start, and I'm pleased to discover that Quin really is taking it easy, and he stops frequently to point out the sights and tell amusing stories. He's actually quite charming and would probably be good on the stage. *Quin McMahan,* I think to myself as we pedal up a small hill; his name even has a theatrical sound to it. Like it's almost familiar. And that's when I remember that my aunt's lost love was Ian

McMahan, and I wonder if Quin could possibly be a relative, although I suspect that McMahan might be a fairly common name over here. Still, it's intriguing.

When we stop for lunch at one, I sit with Darby and a couple of college girls from Melbourne, Australia. When there's a lull in the conversation, I decide to ask Darby about my aunt's deceased ex-boyfriend. "His name was McMahan too," I continue. "Do you think he might've been one of Quin's relatives?"

She laughs. "Probably so, since we all like to believe that everyone in Ireland is related if you go back far enough. But to be truthful, there are a lot of McMahans. Do you know the man's first name by chance?"

"Ian," I tell her. "Ian McMahan. He'd probably be fifty-something by now. Except that he died some time ago."

She seems to be thinking about this. "Ian McMahan?"

"Yes."

"Quin has an uncle named Ian. And he's about the age you mentioned. But he's very much alive."

I shrug. "Must just be a coincidence."

But she's standing up and waving to Quin now, calling him over to us. And I'm embarrassed, thinking that I shouldn't have said anything. It's obvious that if Quin's uncle Ian is alive, he couldn't possibly be my aunt's lost love.

"Quin?" says Darby. "Maddie says her aunt used to be your uncle's girlfriend."

Quin looks confused. "What?"

"Oh no, it can't be the same guy." I try to brush this away. "My aunt's boyfriend died more than twenty years ago." I almost mention the car bomb but then reconsider. I know enough about Ireland by now to understand that IRA attacks aren't exactly comfortable conversation around here. "His name was Ian McMahan," I say quickly, "and I thought that he might possibly have been a relative, but I can see—"

"Are you certain it was *Ian* McMahan?" Quin asks me sharply.

"Yes. But I'm sure it was a *different* Ian McMahan. I'm sorry to trouble you with this. I mean, there must be lots of—"

"No," he says as if he's not ready to let this go. "Let's settle this now. Do you know how your Ian McMahan may have died?"

I glance over my shoulder, and the only ones listening seem to be the Australian girls, although they do seem to be all ears just now. "A car bomb," I say quietly. "Along with another man. I can't recall his first name, but his last name was McIntire."

Quin turns and looks at Darby with a shocked expression. But she just looks confused.

"That was Blair and Michael," he says in quiet voice.

"You mean your uncle Blair?" Her eyes grow wide, as if she's just figured something out.

He nods with a sober expression. But I'm feeling more confused than ever.

"Who are you talking about?" I ask. "Who is Blair and who is Michael?"

"Michael McIntire and Blair McMahan."

"I still don't understand. What does this have to do with Ian?"

"Come," Quin says to me in a gentle voice. "Let's take a dander, shall we?"

"A dander?"

"A wee stroll," he tells me.

I glance at Darby, but she just nods as if this is a good plan. And then Quin leads me over to where a stone wall borders a strip of beach, and we walk alongside of it. "I don't want everyone to overhear this," he tells me. "It's not a very happy story."

"I know," I say. "That's why I felt bad bringing it up. But, still, I don't understand. What does this have to do with Ian?"

"My uncle Blair was Ian's older brother. He was driving Ian's car that day. Taking Michael to the airport. At first everyone believed Ian was driving, since it was his car. The news even reported that it was Ian who'd been killed by the bomb—Ian and Michael. But later on, the truth surfaced. Ian had been down in Dublin that day. I was only a wee lad then, but I remember the stories as well as I remember my name. My father, the oldest of the three brothers, suffered greatly. Our entire family suffered greatly. It was a dark day for everyone."

I'm trying to take this information in. "Do you mean that Ian McMahan is still living?"

"He is."

I shake my head, trying to process this startling news. Like what does this mean? And, more importantly, what will this do to my aunt?

"He lives not far from here. In Derry."

"I think we drove through Derry."

"Aye, I'm sure you did."

"And he's really alive?"

"He is."

"And you think this is really the same Ian McMahan my aunt knew back in the seventies?"

"It seems that way."

We're walking back to the other cyclists now. Darby is looking at her watch and acting like it's time to get this show back on the road again.

"Let's get ready to roll," calls Quin.

"What will I tell my aunt?" I mutter, more to myself than anyone.

"Tell her the truth," says Quin. "That's always the best way."

"Yes." I nod. "Of course."

Then we're packing it up and getting on our bikes, and soon we're all riding again. And while the sights along the way are stunningly beautiful and it's an amazing day for a trek like this, all I can think about is the mysterious Ian McMahan, a person I've never met and never even knew existed until several days ago. And then I thought he was dead. Very confusing. I'm also thinking of all the questions I neglected to ask Quin: Is Ian married? Does he have kids? Was he in the IRA or maybe even the RIRA? Is he a good guy? Or someone we should avoid? But more than anything else, I'm wondering how I'll break this news to Sid. What will she do?

At five o'clock all the cyclists pile onto a small ferryboat that takes us around the bay to see the aquatic marine sights, which prove to be quite fascinating. I am amazed at how clear the water is and how easy it is to see the ocean life below.

We're back in Malin Town at just a little past six, turning in our bikes and thanking Quin and Darby for a wonderful day.

"Don't leave just yet," Quin says to me as I hand him my helmet.

So I stand around and wait as he and Darby check in the bikes and helmets until the last one is finally locked up in the rack behind the small shop.

"I want a word with you before you speak to your aunt," Quin tells me as we go back inside the bike shop.

"This is so incredible," says Darby. "To think that your aunt and Ian were sweethearts, and she thought he'd died. It's like a romance story."

I frown. "Sort of." I can't help but think this story will have a sad or, at the very least, a confusing ending.

"I can give you Ian's telephone number in Derry," says Quin as he looks through a small book on the counter, then writes something down, "if your aunt wishes to look him up."

"Thank you," I say as he hands the slip of paper to me.

"Ian is a decent fellow," Quin says, as if he suspects my concerns. "He's been like a father to me since my own da died several years ago. Ian's the one who loaned me the money to open this shop."

Darby nods. "That's right. Ian is a really nice bloke. I would think you might wish to look him up. Did she ever marry? Your aunt, I mean."

"No. She's actually been single this whole time."

Darby's eyes light up, and she raises her brows as she tosses Quin a glance. "Ian's not married either."

"Really?"

"He was married for a while," Quin informs me. "But she was a real *eejit*, that one."

"I've heard that word here before," I say. "What's an eejit?"

Darby laughs. "An idiot."

"They got married shortly after Ian opened this really posh restaurant in Derry. And it takes a fair amount of time and effort to keep it running well. His wife liked the money just fine, but she was always cheesed off about the work."

"Cheesed off?"

"Angry," offers Darby. "I reckon she thought she was a princess."

"A real *shiver*, she was."

"Huh?"

Darby laughs. "A shiver is someone who's lazy."

I nod. "Oh yeah."

"No one was too surprised when she took off with another bloke. They got a divorce about five years ago."

Quin is shutting down his computer now, and I suspect that he and Darby might like to call it a day. "Can I ask you a question?"

"Ask away," says Quin as he comes over to the other side of the counter.

"Well, was Ian ever involved in the IRA? Or is he still?"

Quin frowns now, as if he's carefully considering his answer. "That's something I couldn't really tell you."

I look down at the floor, feeling embarrassed. "Yes, I probably shouldn't have asked."

Darby pats me on the back. "There are some things best left unsaid."

"We like to think we're a new generation," says Darby, "that we've gotten beyond the old ways…put the troubles behind us, you know?"

I nod.

"Oh, we might just be fooling ourselves," says Quin. "But we do hope for peace."

"Even after what happened in Belfast yesterday?" I ask.

He frowns. "That was a sorry piece of work."

"Maybe it'll be the last," says Darby, but Quin looks doubtful.

"Well, thanks for telling me all that you did." I hold up the slip of paper. "And thanks for Ian's number. My aunt is really going to be shocked."

Darby nudges Quin with her elbow. "Maybe you should go and meet them for a pint. Talk to the aunt, tell her a bit more about Ian."

"Do you think she'd be up for that?" asks Quin as we walk toward the door and he turns off the lights.

"That'd be great," I tell him. "It's going to be hard enough to break this news to her. Having you there to answer questions might be really helpful."

"How about we meet you at Callaghan's?"

"Where's that?" I ask.

"Just a few doors down. Darby's dad owns the place. We live in an apartment just above it."

"Sounds great."

"My brother's working tonight," says Darby. "His name is Tim. Just tell him to ring us, and we'll be down."

"Thanks," I tell them. "I think my aunt should be back at our hotel by now."

So we part ways, but as I head back to the hotel, I feel very disoriented. Like how did this whole thing happen? And why did I just happen to run into Ian's nephew today? And how is Sid going to react? Part of me is excited, but another part of me is worried. In some ways, I wish none of this had happened. Quin's answer to my IRA question wasn't the least bit reassuring. If anything, I think it may mean that Ian is still active in the IRA. And how will my aunt handle that? Perhaps even worse, how will Ryan handle it?

Ten

I don't see Ryan or my aunt when I enter the hotel. And when I tap on their doors, there is no response. I decide to take a shower and clean up. By the time I finish, it's a little after seven, and I'm seriously hungry. I decide to try their rooms again. My aunt still doesn't answer, which worries me a little. What if Molly was an RIRA member? What if they found out about Sid's conversation with Sean? I knock loudly on Ryan's door and am relieved when he opens it.

"Hey, you're there," I say, trying to hide my concerns.

"You missed out on a great day," he tells me.

"Maybe." I try to decide whether to tell him about Ian just yet. "Actually, I had a rather interesting day myself."

"I was about to hop in the shower," he says. "Get rid of some of the fish slime. Is Sid back yet?"

"Not that I know of."

"Well, I'm starving," he says.

"Me too."

"I'll meet you in the lobby in ten minutes," he says.

I wait downstairs, pacing the lobby as I try to decide whether to call my aunt on her cell. I'm afraid I'll spill the beans.

"No sign of Sid?" asks Ryan, coming up behind me.

I turn and shake my head. "I left a message at the desk for her. I told her we'd be at Callaghan's Pub."

"Going pubbing, are we?" he says in a teasing tone.

I give him my slightly narrow-eyed look.

"Sorry." He holds up his hands in defense. "Didn't mean to trip your trigger, Maddie."

"That's not it," I tell him as I head for the door.

"What's up then?"

I don't begin telling him until we're outside. But we're barely a block from the hotel before I've pretty much blurted out the whole story. Well, the nutshell version anyway. I'm saving the details for later.

Ryan actually stops walking, turns and grabs me by the shoulders, and yells, "No way!"

I nod without answering.

"Ian McMahan is alive?"

"According to his nephew Quin McMahan, he is."

Ryan looks totally stunned as he shakes his head. "This is unbelievable, Maddie. Unreal." Then he looks at me with those huge blue eyes. "But if—and I mean *if*—Ian is alive, do you think... Is it possible..."

I know exactly where he's going now. The same thought originally struck me as well. "You're wondering about your dad?" I say in a meek voice.

"Yes!" His eyes light up. "Do you think he could be alive too?"

"I don't really think so, Ryan." Then I tell him about how Ian's brother Blair was driving Ian's car that day. How it was a natural assumption that it was Ian who'd died with Ryan's dad and how it made it to the newspapers and they didn't find out until a day or two later.

"Wow." Ryan takes a deep breath. "This is really freaky, Maddie. I mean, what do you think Sid's going to do when she hears?"

"I have no idea." I point toward the village green. "The pub is over there. Darby's dad owns it."

"Who's Darby?"

So I fill him in a bit on Quin and Darby. And by the time I finish, we're there. "Shall I tell them we're here yet?" I ask Ryan.

"Maybe we should wait for Sid."

So we just sit down, and when Ryan orders a cola, I try not to look too surprised.

"I feel like I stepped into the Twilight Zone today." I try to replay the day's events for him with more detail this time. "Do you think maybe I just dreamed this whole thing?"

He kinda laughs. "Yeah. I'm sure you stayed in the hotel all day and just slept. Right?"

"I sort of wish that was the case."

"To be honest, I'm really worried about how Sid is going to take this."

"Me too." Then I tell him that Ian is single now, and I give him the background story of the lazy wife who ran off with another guy.

"Sounds like Ian's had some rough times."

"But at least he's alive," I say. Although I'm wondering if that's really such a good thing—I mean, as far as my aunt is concerned.

"This really throws a wrench into the works, doesn't it?" Then I tell Ryan about my IRA question.

"I can't believe you actually asked them that."

"I know. It was probably stupid."

The guy working at the bar, probably Darby's brother Tim, is setting our drinks on the wooden table now. He stands over us, studying us, or maybe just me, for what feels like several seconds. And this guy is pretty big and fairly intimidating looking, and I'm wondering if he might possibly be an IRA member himself. What if he overheard me telling Ryan about my concerns over Ian's possible involvement? I am suddenly really nervous.

"You that girl Quin and Darby met today?" he says to me in a rather gruff voice.

I nod and mumble faintly, "Yeah."

Then he smiles, and his whole face lights up. "Drinks are on the house tonight."

I blink. "Well, uh, thanks. Thanks a lot."

"No problem." He nods to a narrow wooden staircase that runs along one side of the bar. "You want me to tell Quin and Darby you're here now?"

"We're still waiting for my aunt," I say.

"Just let me know, and I'll give 'em a holler. By the way, I'm Darby's brother, Tim."

"Thanks," I tell him. Then remembering my manners, I introduce both Ryan and myself to him.

"Welcome to Callaghan's," he tells us. "If you want something to eat, I'll send my wife, Rhiannon, over with the menus."

"Sounds good," I say. "I'm actually starving."

He grins. "You've come to the right place. My ma's the cook, and we've not heard any complaints yet." When he walks away, I wonder why I was such an eejit for being afraid.

"Nice guy," says Ryan.

"Seems like it." Okay, I don't admit I was getting ready to run for my life just now. Or that this whole IRA thing has really got me spooked. I mean, can I help it if I'm a little on the wary side?

"Hey, there's Sid," says Ryan. He stands up and waves toward the door. "She must've gotten your message."

"Sorry to be late," she says as she comes to our table.

"How did it go?" I ask.

She looks pleased. "Okay, I think. Molly seems like a really sweet person. She has three school-aged children and is still very supportive of the peace camps. In fact, her children are all at the camp right now."

"Cool."

"So I think I'll pop into the camp before we go home. Check it out and see how it's changed."

"Sounds good," I say. Then Ryan gives me a look like, *Are you going to tell her now?* And I'm not really sure how to begin.

"This must be your aunt," says Tim as he sets three menus on the table.

She smiles up at him and orders a pint.

"Do you want me to ring Quin and Darby now?" he asks me.

"No," I say quickly. "Why don't we order our dinner first?"

He nods. "Sure. I'll send Rhiannon over in a bit."

"Wow," says my aunt after he leaves. "Looks like you guys know everyone in Malin by now. Fast work, kids."

Ryan nods to me. "It's Maddie who's making all the friends."

I kind of laugh. "Actually, I just met Tim. He's Darby's brother. And Darby is Quin's wife."

"And how did you meet Darby and Quin?"

I briefly tell her of the bike tour around Malin Head.

"That sounds wonderful, Maddie. What a lovely way to spend the day!" She turns to Ryan now. "And how did the fishing go?"

He glances at me. "Uh, fine, Sid."

"So did you catch—"

"Look, Sid," he says, "Maddie has something really *urgent* to tell you."

Sid turns and looks at me now. "Really? This sounds important. Don't tell me that some charming Irishman has swept you off your feet, proposed to you, and now you've decided to stay on in Ireland and—"

"No." I sit up straight and look her in the eyes. "What I have to say is even more startling than that. You might want to brace yourself, Aunt Sid."

Her smile fades. "Not bad news, I hope?"

"Depends." And so I blunder through my story, but when I reach the part where I tell her that Ian McMahan is alive, her face gets pale. "Are you okay?" I ask.

Just then Tim sets her pint on the table. And I can tell by the way he's looking at my aunt that he's heard the whole story by now.

I'm guessing everyone in Darby's and Quin's families have heard the story by now. Maybe the entire town of Malin knows.

Sid takes a swig of stout and then stares at me with intense eyes. "Could you please repeat that last part again, Maddie?"

"Quin McMahan is Ian McMahan's nephew," I say slowly. "He told me it was Blair McMahan, Ian's older brother, who was killed with Ryan's dad that day. It was a temporary case of mistaken identity."

She turns and looks at Ryan almost as if she expects him to dispute this information. But with his lips pressed tightly together, he slowly nods.

Now she looks back at me. I don't think I've ever seen my aunt appear so confused and helpless. It's like she's trying to decide whether to run or scream or maybe even pass out.

I push her stout toward her. "Have another drink."

She frowns at me but does as I say. And I'm relieved to see a woman, who must be Rhiannon, coming toward us. We haven't even looked at our menus, but I suddenly remember a line my aunt uses at times like this.

"What would you recommend?" I ask her.

"Well, we're famous for our fish and chips," she begins.

"That's what I'll have," I say quickly.

"Me too," says Ryan.

"Make that three," says my aunt, although I suspect her food may go untouched again tonight.

After Rhiannon leaves, I reach over and put my hand on my aunt's. Hers is quite cool. "Are you okay?" I ask again.

Her eyes are slightly glassy as she stares across the table, just looking out into space. "I'm in shock," she finally says.

I'm not sure how much I should tell her. But then I figure if she's already in shock, maybe it's best to get this over with as quickly as possible. Kind of like being at the dentist. Quicker is usually better. So I tell the rest of the story—how Ian was married, but it didn't work out, and now he runs a nice restaurant in Derry, and both Darby and Quin think he's a really great guy. "I even have his phone number." I dig in my purse for the slip of paper Quin gave me and hand it to her.

Without speaking, she just stares blankly at the numerals.

"And you might as well know," I finally say, "I asked them if Ian was still involved in the IRA."

Her blue eyes flash with something now. I'm not sure if it's anger or fear or what. "You didn't," she says in a quiet voice.

"Yeah, I did." I make a face. "I know it was really, really dumb. What can I say, Sid, except that I'm a great big eejit?"

My admission almost makes her smile. "Well, I'm sure they didn't reveal anything to you one way or the other."

"No, of course not."

It's not long before our fish and chips arrive, and although I was starving earlier, I'm not feeling too hungry just now. But Ryan generously sprinkles malt vinegar over his and immediately digs in. "Hey, these are really good, you guys. You might want to eat them while they're hot."

I decide to take a bite. "No wonder they're famous for this," I say.

Just as we're finishing up, Tim comes back again. "Do you want me to ring Quin and Darby yet?"

I glance at my aunt, and she just nods.

"Sure," I tell Tim. "Thanks."

He tips his head slightly, as if to show he understands that this isn't easy for any of us. And after a few minutes, Quin and Darby show up. I make more introductions, including an explanation about Ryan's connection to Ian, and Tim brings an extra chair for them to join us.

"Can I get you some dessert?" he asks. "Ma's got a blueberry cobbler fresh from the oven."

We all decide to have some, and Tim tells Rhiannon to get it for us, along with some coffee Sid requested.

"This is all so shocking," my aunt says to Darby and Quin. "The news that Ian is alive. It's almost unbelievable."

"It's true," says Quin. "Ian is alive and well. And I hope you don't mind, but I rang him up after we got home tonight."

"It was my idea," Darby says quickly. "I thought he deserved to know that you're here."

Sid blinks and sits up straighter. "And how did he react?"

"He'd like to see you," says Quin.

"Well, I…"

"But only if you want," adds Darby. "He doesn't want to force it."

"That's right," says Quin. "I think he feels bad for, uh, for how it went with you two all those years ago."

Sid gives him what is obviously a forced smile. "Oh, that was long ago," she says just a little too casually. "Water under the bridge, really."

Quin tips his head toward Ryan. "He'd like to meet Ryan too."

"Why's that?" she asks, her eyes suspicious.

"As you know, Ian and Michael were close friends. Ian would like to see Michael's only son."

"Oh yes." Sid gives a stiff nod. "Of course."

"He's willing to come here if that's better for you."

Sid seems to consider this, but I can tell she's already made up her mind. "That won't work. We'll be leaving Malin tomorrow. I have some business to attend to."

"Maybe you could stop and see him in Derry," suggests Darby hopefully. "It's on the way."

"Perhaps." Sid looks away, and I have a feeling she's just trying to placate them, like she wants to end this conversation and the sooner the better.

"Ian would really appreciate that," says Darby a little eagerly. I suspect by the look in her eyes that she's still expecting a storybook ending to this romantic little tale. But I think it's highly unlikely. I can tell by how Sid's acting that she's not looking forward to this meeting at all, and it wouldn't surprise me if she figures out a way to avoid it altogether.

We eat our dessert and visit with Quin and Darby about lots of other things—like how Malin won a tidy-town award, and how it's the sunniest spot in all of Ireland, and how Quin has developed a thriving bicycle business over recent years.

"It's been a pleasure to meet you," my aunt says as she reaches for her purse. "But I've had a very long day, and I'm afraid I'm starting to fade. Do you mind if I excuse myself?"

"Of course not," says Quin as he stands. "I'm glad we got acquainted. And I hope you'll take the time to see my uncle."

"Please let us know how it goes," says Darby. Her eyes are on me now, like she thinks I'm the only one who can keep her posted on future developments. But I'm not sure I want to.

"Thank you for meeting with us," says my aunt in a formal voice. "May I get the check now, please?"

"Oh no," says Darby quickly. "It's on the house tonight."

"But I—"

"We insist," says Quin.

"Well, thank you," says Sid. She looks slightly off guard now. "That's very generous of you."

"Just Irish hospitality." Darby grins at us. "After all, you're almost like family."

I can see Sid bristle at that comment, but the congenial smile remains plastered on her face, and she thanks them once again.

It's dark as we walk toward the hotel. No one is saying anything. And I feel responsible for this whole nightmare. I'm the one who brought this unexpected pain to my aunt. And I feel really guilty.

"I'm so sorry, Sid," I blurt out. "I shouldn't have—"

"No," she says, turning to face me. "This isn't your fault, Maddie. Please, don't apologize. And once I recover from the shock, well, I think I should be happy, at least for Ian's sake…I mean, that he's alive. That's something, isn't it?"

But I know what she's thinking. If he's alive, why did he never contact her again? Was it because the romance really was over and done with? And yet she spent all those years thinking he was dead. Would it have gone differently for her if she'd known he was alive? Or am I just imagining things, blowing this all out of proportion?

"I think this is a God thing," Ryan says when we stop in front of the door of the hotel.

"Really?" My aunt turns and stares at him. I'm not sure if it's the shadows from the streetlight or if she is really angry now. But I'm thinking the latter.

He nods with enthusiasm. "Yeah. I think so. I really think God planned for Maddie to take that bike tour just so she could meet Quin and find out about Ian. And I think God wants you to see Ian again and—"

"What if I do *not* want to see him?" she demands.

"Why wouldn't you?" he asks innocently, and I'm glad it's Ryan, not me, doing the asking, because Sid is seething now.

"Why wouldn't I?" Her voice gets louder, and I'm glad no one's around to overhear us. "After thirty years of believing he was dead, thirty years of not hearing a word from him, you're asking me why I do not want to see him again? Why should I *want* to see him, Ryan?"

He just shrugs, but I can tell by his expression, he's taking this personally.

"Whatever happened then is over with now!" she actually yells. "And I'd appreciate it if I never heard his name again! Thank you very much!" And then she turns and storms into the hotel. I've never seen my aunt lose her temper like this. Seriously, I always thought she was the cool aunt, the one who never got ruffled. I'm a little shocked.

Ryan and I remain outside, just standing on the sidewalk in front of the closed door. And suddenly I feel really, really bad for him. He looks kind of crushed, and I know she hurt his feelings. And it makes me pretty mad. I mean, he didn't deserve that. Ryan's been such a good sport about everything on this trip. He's been patient with me, helpful and supportive to Sid. For her to treat him that way was totally uncalled for.

I reach over and put my hand on his arm. "She's just really upset," I say, as if that's not obvious. "She didn't mean to—"

"It's okay." He shoves his hands into his jeans pockets and looks away. "I understand…"

And we just stand there for a couple of minutes.

"Want to talk about it?" I ask in a slightly timid voice.

He doesn't answer.

"Can I buy you a pint?" I offer, feeling kind of silly but desperate. I hate seeing him like this.

He looks at me, then kind of smiles. "Never expected to hear that from you, Maddie."

"People change," I say as I take his arm and lead him to the pub attached to our hotel.

Ryan stops short of the entrance. "Hey, do you think they have cocoa? I feel like something warm and chocolaty."

I giggle and shrug. "Guess we could ask." We get seated in a quiet corner, order our Irish cocoas, and I wait for him to say something else. Anything.

"I want to meet him," he finally says.

"Who?" I glance around the room expecting to see someone of interest.

"Ian."

"Oh yeah." *Earth to Maddie,* I tell myself. *Keep up.*

"He and my dad were really good friends, Maddie."

I nod. "Yeah."

"And I never knew my dad…"

"And meeting Ian could be a connection for you."

"I really do think it's a God thing."

"I do too, Ryan. But maybe it's more for you than Sid."

"I guess."

"I mean, you can't really blame her. Ian must've meant more than anyone knows to her. Think about it: she never married…and did you see her face tonight? I've never seen her like that. I don't think she ever got over him."

"But it's been thirty years."

"I know, and I don't get it. But I think it's true. Why else would she react like she did?"

"Yeah, you're probably right. Now that I think about it, she has been acting kind of strange during this trip."

"Like she's been haunted by the past," I suggest.

"I actually wondered if it was Ian's ghost."

"But now we know he's alive."

"I know it's going to be hard on her…" He looks up at me with determination. "But somehow I've got to meet him, Maddie."

"I know."

"Even if I have to do it without her knowing."

"I'll help you, Ryan. Somehow we'll get you and Ian together."

When I replay these words later on, back in my hotel room, I realize that they sound very much like a promise. And I wonder how I could possibly have made a commitment like that. How can I force a meeting that my aunt is so diametrically opposed to? After all, this is really her trip. She's the one who invited us, and she's paying for everything. And she's the only one who can drive the rental car. How fair is it for me to insist on seeing someone she may actually wish were dead? Okay, that's a bit harsh, but I know she wishes that he hadn't popped back into her life like this. And I know she'll do everything to avoid seeing him.

But just the same, I'll do everything I can to see that Ryan gets to meet Ian. How can I not? Ryan is right. I think this truly is a God thing. And when I go to bed later that night, I really pray.

First I pray for Ryan. I ask God to restore this old broken connection that links him to his father. I ask God to use Ian to give Ryan some answers to his questions and find some resolution for the loss of his dad. And I pray for Sid too. That's a little harder. But I ask God to use this dilemma with Ian to bring about some healing in her heart. Some kind of closure. Somehow I think that's what she needs.

As for me, well, I just pray God will help me to continue to grow up—and not be such an eejit!

Eleven

wake up early again. I'm not sure what's up with this but decide that maybe I've turned into a morning person—or maybe it's just being in Ireland. I get up and get dressed, but instead of going downstairs, I go ahead and get my stuff packed. I haven't forgotten my aunt's announcement last night that we're leaving Malin today. Okay, I'm not thrilled with her decision, but who am I to argue? Just as I'm zipping my last bag, I hear a light tapping on my door.

"Maddie?" calls my aunt.

I open the door to see Sid standing in the hallway. Not looking her best, she's wearing a baggy green cardigan over her Scottie-dog flannel pajamas, and her eyes are red and puffy.

"You okay?" I ask.

She shrugs.

"Wanna come in?" I open the door wider and wave her inside. I'm not sure I want anyone in the hotel seeing her like this.

She looks around my tidy room. "You're packed?"

I nod. "Figured I might as well."

"Oh." She looks slightly confused.

"You said we were leaving, Sid."

"That's right." She sits down on my bed, shoulders hunched in a dejected heap of flannel and wool. I sit in the side chair across from her, cross my legs, lean back, and wait.

She sits up straighter, using both hands to push her hair away from her face. But the mussed-up strands fall back in a heap. Then she lets out a deep sigh that seems laced with pain.

"I know this Ian thing is hard on you," I begin carefully. "And I can't even begin to imagine what it would feel like to be in your shoes. In fact, I'm sure I'd be totally freaking."

"You got that right."

"But I also think it's really important for Ryan to meet him. I mean, think about it. Ian is like the last connection to Ryan's dad. Can you imagine what that might mean to Ryan? He's never even known his dad. And you know that Danielle hardly ever spoke of him, not until just before she died, and that wasn't much. Besides, you said yourself that you brought Ryan over here to trace his family's—"

"Ian is *not* part of Ryan's family."

"But he is a connection to Ryan's dad. A very strong connection. That might be more important than being related."

She closes her eyes and leans her head back.

"How about if we stay in Malin just one more day?" I plead with her. "Just like you originally planned. And maybe you can do another interview or some research or something…" I'm creating this plan as I speak. "And maybe Ryan and I could meet with Ian right here in town. Like at Callaghan's. And you could be off somewhere else far away. We could make your excuses for you—say you're really busy gathering material for your articles and you've got lots to do and stuff."

She opens her eyes now, and pressing her fingers on either side of her temples, she actually seems to be considering my half-hatched plan. "I guess that would be okay, Maddie."

"Really?" I stand up in excitement.

"Yeah." She stands up too. "What can it hurt?"

I throw my arms around her. "Thanks, Sid. That's really great of you."

"As long as you promise to leave me totally out of it."

I hold up three fingers in the old Girl Scout pledge. "I promise."

"And I do have another interview I can do today. Molly told me about a friend of hers who was at the peace camp a year or two after Danielle and I were there. She lives in Buncrana, which isn't too far from here. I'll give her a call and see if I can stop in. And if not, I'll just do a little sightseeing along the coastline. I've always heard Malin Head is a must-see."

"It definitely is," I assure her. "To be honest, I was kind of distracted yesterday, but everything I saw was amazing."

"Yeah, I imagine I'll be kind of distracted too."

I hug her again. "I'm so sorry about this, Sid. I wish this wasn't so hard on you."

"Me too."

Then she goes back to her room, and I go quietly knock on Ryan's door. When he doesn't answer, my first reaction is to worry. I mean, he did seem pretty bummed last night. Then I realize he probably just got up early and went out to get some breakfast. So I head over to town and end up in the same bakery as yesterday. And there he is, standing at the counter, ordering his breakfast.

"Great minds again," I say as I step up behind him.

"Check out today's breakfast special." He points to the blackboard. "An Irish Fry."

"Sounds good to me."

We take our coffees over to a table, and I tell him the good news.

"Seriously?"

I nod. "Yep. She's giving us today to meet Ian."

"That is so cool. And there's a pay phone right outside. Should I go call him now?"

I slap my forehead. "I gave his number to Sid."

"Do you think she's left?"

"I hate to bug her," I say. "Especially for Ian's number. Kind of like rubbing salt in the wound. I'll just get it from Quin again."

So we finish our breakfast and head for the bike shop, which fortunately opens early. The little bell on the door dings merrily as we go inside.

"Booking another tour, are you?" Darby greets us with a bright smile.

"No thanks," I say. "I just need to get Ian's number again."

"So you're going to give him a ring after all?" She looks hopeful.

"Ryan's going to call him," I explain as she writes down the number. "My aunt, well, she needs to think about it. And she has some interview stuff to do today. You know, she's really here in Ireland on assignment." Okay, that's the best I can do without actually lying. Although I'm sure Darby has her own suspicions.

"Why don't you just ring him from here?" suggests Darby. "Quin won't mind. And if you need privacy, you can use the telephone in the back room."

Ryan thanks her, then follows her back while I amuse myself by checking out their rack of Ireland tourism pamphlets.

"Quin's delivering some bicycles over to the resort at Malin Head," Darby tells me when she returns. "But he should be back soon."

"Are you guys doing another tour today?" I ask.

"Not on Sundays."

"That's right. I've sort of lost track of the days since we got here."

"How long have you been in Ireland?"

I do the mental math. "This is our sixth day," I tell her. "Wow, that means we only have a week left."

"Make the most of it."

I hold up a pamphlet that's promoting castle tours in Donegal. "Is this any good?"

She crinkles up her nose. "Rather pricey for what they offer. You can just as easily do that yourself and take as much time as you like. Plus you can skip some of the less interesting castles." She points to a name. "Like that one. I don't know why anyone would pay to see it."

I make a mental note.

"So where will you be heading from here?" she asks.

"Northern Ireland. Belfast, I think."

She frowns. "Why do you want to go there?"

"For my aunt's research."

"Oh. I'm not trying to say it's not an interesting place. But my family comes from there, and we were all quite relieved to get away. Now you couldn't pay me to go back and visit."

"Hello," calls Quin as he comes into the shop, wheeling a bike with a flat tire. "Nice to see you again, Maddie."

"Ryan's using the telephone in the back room," Darby warns him. "Ringing your uncle."

Quin's eyes light up. "Good to hear."

"Yes, my aunt's got some business to take care of," I say quickly, "but Ryan and I thought maybe Ian would want to drive over here—to meet Ryan, you know, since his father was a good friend of Ian's."

"I'm sure he'll be glad to."

"It's set," says Ryan as he emerges from the back room. "Ian will be here around noon. We'll meet him at Callaghan's."

"Good choice," says Darby. Then she looks at her watch. "We'd better be off if we're going to make it to Mass." She glances at us. "Care to join us?"

I look at Ryan, and he shrugs. "Why not?"

"Okay," I say. Then I look down at my khaki Capri pants. "But do I need to change?"

Darby steps out from behind the counter to show that she's wearing jeans. "Our church is rather modern about clothes. And you don't need to have your head covered either."

"Oh." So we wait for Quin to close up shop and adjust the clock on the We'll Be Back door sign. Then we follow them across the village green and down a few blocks until we get to an old stone building. The sign out front says Saint Patrick's Reformed Charismatic Catholic Church.

"Long name," I observe.

Quin laughs. "Yeah, it's been changed a few times over the years, but I think they've finally settled on this. We just call it Saint Paddy's."

I've never been to a Catholic church before, but I have been to my grandma's Episcopal church, and I'm guessing they may be similar—although you're not allowed to wear pants to my grandma's church. But I'm preparing myself for group readings and the whole sit-down, stand-up routine that usually catches me off guard. My theory is that it's to keep people from falling asleep in the pews.

But I'm surprised that the music in here is fairly lively. The people sing like they mean it. And the priest gives what I think is a good sermon. Other than communion, which Ryan tells me we probably shouldn't do since we're not actual members of their church, I'm thinking it's not so very different from my church back home.

"That was pretty cool," I tell Quin and Darby as we leave the building.

"Thanks," says Quin. "We like it."

"I thought Catholic churches were supposed to be a lot different from Protestant ones," I say as we meander across the village green.

"Some of them are," says Darby. "I grew up going to a traditional Roman Catholic church in Belfast, and it wasn't anything
like Saint Paddy's."

"I went to a Catholic church with my paternal grandparents
a few times when I was growing up," Ryan tells us. "But I never
understood half of what was going on."

"It makes me wonder what the big deal is," I say as we stop on
the edge of the green. "I mean, why do Christians have so many de-
nominations? And why can't Catholics and Protestants get along?"

"Wouldn't we like to know," says Darby.

"Anyone who comes up with the answer to those questions can
probably rule the world," says Quin.

"Well, it must make God sad to see his children fighting over
religion," I say. "Too bad we can't all just love one another."

"I'm with you on that, Maddie." Darby pats me on the back
and then starts singing the old Beatles song. "All we are saying…is
give peace a chance."

We join her, but other than that one line, none of us can remember the lyrics. I guess that's apropos in an ironic sort of way.

"Well, I better get back to the old grindstone," says Quin.

"It was lovely having you at church with us," adds Darby. "You
will let us know how you get on with Quin's uncle, won't you,
Ryan?"

"Sure," he promises. "Thanks for helping us to connect with
him."

"Tell him hello for me," calls Quin. "And if he has time, perhaps he can drop into the shop later."

"Will do," says Ryan.

"They are so nice," I say as we watch them walk away.

Ryan nods. "They feel almost like family."

"I know what you mean."

He glances at his watch. "We still have about an hour before Ian gets here. Anything you'd like to do?"

I consider this. "Well, there was a music store I wanted to check out. But they were closed yesterday. You think there's any chance they'd be open on a Sunday?"

"This is a tourist town," he says. "Let's go see."

So I guide us to the shop, but it looks dark inside. I decide to give the door a try anyway, and to my pleasant surprise it's unlocked. "It is open," I say as we walk in and look around the dimly lit store.

"Aye, we are," says a man's voice from a dark corner in the back.

"Oh!" I jump and grab Ryan's arm.

"I just unlocked the place," the man says as he switches on the lights. "Is that better?"

"Thanks." Ryan smiles at the old man, who's coming toward us now.

"I came by yesterday, and you were closed," I tell him. "I thought maybe you'd—"

"'Twas closed for my mum's funeral," he says in a sad voice.

"I'm sorry," I tell him. But I'm thinking this old guy, with his white hair and scraggly beard, could be pushing eighty himself. His mother must've been ancient.

"Me mum was nearly one hundred," he tells us. "Blind as a bat and deaf as a doorknob. But she was a dear saint all the same, God rest her soul. Now what can I show you two fine young things?"

"I'm interested in an Irish drum," Ryan tells him. And just like that the old guy sweeps Ryan off to a wall where all sorts of flat, tambourine-shaped drums are hanging. The smallest are not much bigger than a tambourine, and the largest must be nearly three feet wide. Before long they are playing the drums, and it sounds like a Native American powwow.

I go to the other side of the store, where I noticed a display of flutes when we came in. I used to play the flute but gave it up in exchange for my guitar. Still, I've enjoyed the sounds of the Irish bands and what they call their "penny whistles," and I'm curious as to whether I still remember how to play.

"Is it okay if I try some of these flutes?" I call out when there's a brief reprieve from the drumming.

"Aye, lassie. Make yourself a' home." And then the drumming starts again.

I pick up a penny whistle, which doesn't look too much different from a flute, except that it's smaller and runs vertically instead of horizontally. I place my fingers over the holes and blow. Not bad. I play a few notes and actually impress myself. Then I try a few more for tonal quality. And finally I pick up one of the larger ones. Made of plastic, this one plays a low D, which is lower than smaller metal whistles. I really like the rich, mellow sound and am pleased to see it's only twenty-five euros, and that includes accessories and a songbook. I play on it a bit more, almost forgetting where I am and that I haven't actually purchased it yet. Then I hear a soft drumming sound, almost in accompaniment to what I'm playing. I turn around to see Ryan with a midsize drum, and he's grinning as he plays along with my melody. When we finish, the old man claps with vigor.

"You two are a pair," he says. "You must have Irish in your blood."

Ryan nods and sticks out his hand. "Name's McIntire, and my clan comes from these parts."

"McIntire?" The old man scratches the thin pale whiskers on his chin as if to jog his memory. "Aye, that's a name I know. Large family—mostly boys as I recall—and I knew only a few of them. Frankie McIntire was a schoolmate of mine, but he died a few years back. And then there was his older brother, Glen, who's also passed on…and then, o' course, there was the younger brother, the one who went off to America."

"John?"

"Aye, I believe it was a Johnny McIntire. Him and his wife went off just before the second war."

"My grandfather's name was John."

Now the old man frowns, as if he's remembering something else, something not so pleasant. "No, no," he says, "surely not the same John." He shakes his head sadly. "Not *that* John McIntire."

But Ryan continues. "That John McIntire had a son named Michael."

The old man makes a tsk-tsk sound with his teeth as he looks at Ryan. "Would that be your da, son?"

Ryan nods. "I never knew him."

The old man puts a hand on his shoulder. " 'Tis a shame, son."

There's a long uncomfortable silence, which I try to think of a way to break into. "Why do they call these flutes penny whistles?" I finally ask.

The old man looks relieved as he picks up a small metal whistle and examines it. "No one knows for sure, lassie, but some say it's because of Robert Clarke, the man credited with introducing them to Ireland. They say he sold them for a penny apiece. Others say it's because the poor musicians would play them on the street in the hopes that pennies would be tossed in their direction." Now he grins at me. "You could probably earn a bit o' change yourself playing a fipple flute."

"Fipple flute?" I repeat.

"Another name for a penny whistle."

"Well, I don't know if anyone would throw spare change at me," I say, "unless they were trying to get me to stop playing, but I'd like to buy this anyway."

"And I'm getting this drum," Ryan announces.

"Glad I opened up me shop today," the old man says as he makes his way back behind the counter.

Without the aid of a computer or even a cash register, it takes him several minutes to write each of our purchases on a small receipt pad. We pay him, and he carefully counts out our change. "I'm still not used to this strange-looking currency," he says with a trace of sadness. "I miss the old harps."

"But some of the euros have them," I say.

"Aye, but it's not the same. The world is changing. Ireland is changing."

"But at least your music stays pretty much the same," I say with optimism.

A smile slowly lights his face. "Aye. That's something ya can count on. We'll always have our music."

Then we thank him and head for the door.

"Make beautiful music together," he calls out as we leave.

Ryan just laughs. But I try to hide my embarrassment at what seems an obvious insinuation that we are a couple.

"We better get over to Callaghan's," he says. "It's almost twelve."

"Are you sure you want me with you?" I ask as we head for the green. "I mean, I don't really have any connection with Ian and—"

"I *want* you with me, Maddie. Like it or not, you are a part of this." Then he turns and looks at me with a sincere expression. "Are you okay with that?"

I nod vigorously. "No problem. I can't wait to meet Sid's one true love."

Twelve

I can't believe my palms are sweating as Ryan and I sit at a table in Callaghan's, waiting for Ian to arrive.

"What do you think he looks like?" Ryan says suddenly.

"I have no idea. Maybe you should've asked him to wear a red carnation in his lapel."

Ryan kind of laughs.

"He must be old," I say. "At least older than Sid, I'm guessing. Maybe like my dad's age." I imagine my partially bald dad with his slight potbelly, and while he's not exactly hunk material, he's a sweet guy, and I actually miss him.

"There's a man coming in," Ryan says.

I turn to see a dark-haired man standing in the doorway. It's hard to tell what he looks like with the sun pouring in from behind him, but he looks tall and nicely built.

"Hello, Ian," calls Tim from the bar.

"Tim." Ian waves and goes over toward him. "I'm supposed to meet—"

"I'm Ryan McIntire," Ryan is saying to Ian. I have no idea how he got up and over there so quickly, but I'm right on his heels. "And this is Maddie Chase."

"Ryan and Maddie." Ian looks at us carefully as he shakes our hands. "Pleasure to meet you both."

"We have a table over here," Ryan says, and I can tell he's nervous as he nods to where we'd been sitting with our drinks still barely touched. "Can I buy you a pint?"

"Not for me," says Ian.

"Having your regular, are ya?" Tim says from behind the bar.

"Thank you," Ian calls back as we sit down. Within seconds Tim is bringing over a bottle of lemon soda and a glass, just like I have. "Ol' Ian gave up the stronger stuff a long time ago," he says as he plunks these down in front of him.

"That's right," Ian says almost apologetically. "But I've no problem with others enjoying a pint. I had to learn the hard way it wasn't a good thing for me."

I study this guy as he makes small talk with Ryan, inquiring about what we've seen so far, how long we've been in Ireland, how long we plan to stay, just light stuff. He has neatly cut, almost black hair with a bit of gray at the temples; deep blue eyes with an intensity that's hard to ignore; a firm, straight nose; and a nice, even mouth. For an old dude, Ian is pretty cute.

"And how about you?" he's asking me now.

"What?" I say, feeling stupid for not keeping up.

"How do you like our fair Emerald Isle?"

"Oh, I love it. I totally love it. I think I could live here."

He smiles, which makes the tiny lines at the edges of his eyes fan out in a very attractive way. No wonder Sid had it so bad for this guy!

We talk some more, and it's hard not to notice that he doesn't mention Sid once. I mean, he doesn't even ask where she is or why she's not here. And to be perfectly honest, this bothers me. A lot. Like has he forgotten her completely? Or maybe he never cared for her the way she did for him and is just as glad she's not here. But at least he could ask about her, just for politeness' sake. I'm tempted to bring her up, just to see how he reacts, but I remember my promise to her—to leave her out of this. And so I do.

Our conversation pauses when Rhiannon comes over to take our lunch order. My stomach is feeling pretty tight and twisted just now, so I simply order soup. But Ian and Ryan, who really seem to be hitting it off, decide to have the halibut special.

"Good choice," Rhiannon tells them.

And then she leaves, and the conversation turns serious.

"Your father was a good friend to me," Ian tells Ryan in a sober tone. "I felt like I lost two brothers that day—both Blair and Mickey."

"Mickey?" I say, slightly confused.

"Michael," Ian says. "We were friends for several years, ever since he saved my neck, but right from the beginning I called him Mickey or Mick."

"Saved your neck?" Ryan's brows lift with interest.

"We were both working in construction back then. A large medical building in downtown Belfast. I stepped onto a beam that hadn't been properly secured, and it started to go, but your da reached out and grabbed me by the arm, pulled me back onto the platform, just like that." He snaps his fingers. "Your da saved me from plunging six stories straight down. I'm sure it would've killed me. I owed him after that. And we became best friends."

"Wow." Ryan looks impressed.

"Yeah, that's how I felt too."

"But I'm curious why you weren't with my dad that last day," Ryan says. "Why was your brother driving your car instead of you?"

"I thought I was going to drive Mickey to the airport," Ian says. "I'd actually planned on it. But then a friend rang up at the last moment, asking me to drive a van to…" He pauses now, as if trying to decide how much to say. "To Antrim."

Ryan frowns. "So you drove a van to a place in Antrim instead of driving my dad to the airport."

"I took Mickey out for breakfast quite early that morning," he continues. "Him and Blair both. I'd already asked Blair to use my car to drive Mickey, and they were both fine with that. I said my good-byes." His voice chokes a little. "I just didn't know they were going to be my last good-byes."

"And then you drove a van to Antrim?" For some reason, Ryan seems to be stuck on this small fact. I'm not sure why, but he's so persistent that he almost appears rude.

"That's right," Ian calmly responds.

"Why?" Ryan asks. "It seems to me that if Mickey really was your best friend, and he'd saved your life, and now he was going back to America, you would have at least wanted to see him off at the airport."

Ian nods. "Of course. I *did* want to see him off. But at the time I was feeling a bit torn."

"Torn?"

"You see, Mickey had been gone a few years by then. He'd married Danielle and had a child"—he tips his head to Ryan—"and when Mick left Ireland, well, shall we just say he left some trouble behind as well."

"What kind of trouble?" Ryan persists.

"Let's just say Mickey could've been behind bars had he not chosen to leave."

Ryan seems somewhat defeated now. "Yeah, my mom mentioned something about that."

"How is your mum anyway?"

"She got cancer…" Ryan picks up a fork and stares at it.

I fill in the additional information. "Danielle died last winter."

"Oh no." Ian shakes his head. "I'm so sorry, Ryan. So terribly sorry to hear that. Danielle…she was a fine woman."

Ryan sort of nods. "But back to that day, if you don't mind."

"Not at all."

"You say my dad left Ireland to escape prison, and I know that's true. But why would that change your friendship with him? I don't get it."

"After Mickey left for America, I did some thinking. I sort of reevaluated my life, and I didn't like what I saw. I thought it was time to grow up, move on, you know?"

"And then my dad came back?"

"That's right. And even though I was glad to see him and we spent some good times together, well, I didn't want to return to the past."

"Was my dad a *bad* man?" Ryan asks. I can see the troubled look in his eyes, as if he's always suspected the very worst and now thinks he's about to find out it's true.

"No, no." Ian firmly shakes his head. "Not at all. Mickey was a good man, Ryan. A very good man. But he was passionate. Mickey was the one who could get us going. A true leader, Mickey was. He knew that things were wrong in our country, and he wanted to fix them. Mick was fervent and zealous. He'd get ahold of something, and you'd think he'd never let go." Ian makes a tight fist as if to prove this point.

"So he was obsessed with it?" Ryan asks.

"Obsessed?" Ian considers this word. "Perhaps…"

"Oh."

"But then he met Danielle." Ian smiles. "Oh, she was lovely. And poor Mick was over the moon for her."

Ryan brightens a little. "Yeah, I've heard that."

"Mickey fell completely in love with her. I'd never seen him like that for any girl. And as passionate as he'd been for, well, politics, he became equally passionate for Danielle. I think he would've done anything for her."

"Including leaving Ireland."

"That's right."

"Did you stay in touch with him after he left?"

"A bit. Although neither of us was much on letter writing."

"But he did contact you before he came back here?"

"Actually, it was a mutual friend who told me."

"So you knew he was coming?"

"Of course."

"But something was wrong between you and him?"

Ryan reminds me of a prosecuting attorney just now, like he's trying to make some specific point, but I'm not sure what it is. I wonder if he knows himself.

"Like I said, I'd been trying to distance myself," Ian patiently explains. "From my political ties, so to speak."

"From the IRA?" Ryan says.

"Yes. I'd come to realize that our methods weren't working— that violence only begets violence, and killing just leads to more killing. And innocent people get hurt. It becomes a never-ending vicious cycle. Can you understand that, Ryan?"

It's hard to read Ryan's expression, but he gives a small nod.

"So you were giving it all up then?" It feels like my chance to finally jump in here. "You had really decided to quit"—I lower my voice out of respect for Ian—"the IRA?"

"That's right."

"And then Ryan's dad came back here," I continue, eager to tie this thing up, "but things had changed between you two. He was still involved, but you had moved on."

"That sums it up."

I look at Ryan, hoping this will help him to let go of this… whatever it is he keeps hanging on to. But he still looks slightly troubled.

"So, Ryan." Ian's voice gets lighter. "Have you had a chance to meet any of your relatives yet?"

Ryan's face brightens a bit. "Relatives? I didn't know if any of them were still around." Then he tells Ian about the old man in the music store. "The only ones he knew all seemed to be dead."

"I didn't know many of Mick's relatives," Ian admits. "But there was a spinster aunt in these parts that Mick would visit from time to time, and he took me to meet her once. She was the oldest sibling of the McIntires, his da's only sister. I'm not sure if she's still around or not, but she'd probably be in her eighties by now. She had a little cottage up Malin Head way. As I recall, the home had been in the McIntire family for some time. A bit of history, you know. We could take a ride up there if you like. I could at least show you the spot."

"That'd be great." Ryan smiles now, and I'm hoping we're finished with the subject of Ryan's dad and anything to do with the IRA. It makes me very uncomfortable, and I suspect Ian doesn't care for it much either. I think he's actually been quite patient with Ryan's little inquisition.

"Here ya go," says Rhiannon as she begins to unload a large tray of food. "Eat up."

Thankfully, our conversation does move on now. Ian talks about Quin and how he started the bike shop with practically nothing but in recent years had built it into a thriving operation. "That Quin has quite a good business head on him. He even designed a very clever Web site that he uses to advertise and book his bike tours. It's accessible from all around the world."

"Quin mentioned how you helped him get the shop started," I say as I reach for another piece of soda bread to go with my soup.

"Aw, it wasn't much that I did. And I was happy to help him. Quin's been the closest thing to a son for me."

For some reason this reminds me of Sid. And, of course, there are so many questions I'd love to ask Ian. But for my aunt's sake, I will keep my mouth shut. Still, I keep wishing he'd ask about her. Just once. Like, "How's old Sid doing these days?" Some casual little reminder that he actually remembers her name. It kills me to think she's been pining away for a guy who won't even give her the time of day. It's so wrong.

"Quin said to stop by the shop if you have time today," Ryan says as we're leaving the pub.

"Of course. I wouldn't think of leaving town without doing that." Ian looks at his watch. "Do you still want to go see the cottage?"

"Definitely." Ryan glances at me. "Do you want to come too?"

"Sure."

"How about if I pick you up at half past two?" Ian suggests.

So we tell him which hotel we're in, and it's settled.

"He seems nice," I say to Ryan as we walk back to the hotel.

"I guess."

"You don't like him?"

"I don't really know him."

"But he answered all your questions," I remind him.

"Sort of."

"Is it hard letting go of this thing with your dad?"

"Letting go?" He tosses me a curious glance.

"I mean, it seems you're kind of hanging on to something. Like there's something in your dad's past you can't get over."

"Well, it's been pretty weird hearing that the guy who was supposed to be my dad's best friend in Ireland, the guy who was supposed to have been killed with my dad, is still alive. Not only that, but he gave up on the cause my dad died for. And did you hear his excuse, Maddie?"

"Driving the van?"

"Yeah. What's up with that?"

"I think it was just his way of distancing himself from your dad," I say as we reach the hotel. "Keeping himself separate from anything to do with the IRA."

"Yeah, but then my dad gets blown up, Maddie. Does that seem a little fishy to you?"

"But Ian's brother was blown up with him, Ryan. And Ian's car too."

"That certainly made it *look* innocent."

"Ryan?" I study him for a moment, wondering what happened to the Ryan I thought I knew. The grounded guy with an answer for everything.

"I know, I know," he says as he reaches for the door. "I probably sound paranoid. But I guess I just need to get to the bottom of this."

"What if there is no bottom?"

He shrugs as we go inside. "I suppose that's a real possibility."

"So, tell me," I say after we're upstairs and about to part ways.

"Are you going to keep grilling Ian when he drives us to Malin Head?"

"I don't know."

"You are, aren't you?"

"Maybe. Why?"

I consider this as I try to find my room key in my bag. "Because if that's the case, I'm not sure I want to go with you. I mean, it was pretty uncomfortable during lunch."

"Sorry."

"No, that's okay. I actually sort of understand, Ryan. And if this is something you just need to get out of your system, well then, be my guest. I guess I'm saying I don't want to be a willing participant." I don't add that it also makes me feel pretty sorry for Ian.

"Okay, what if I promise to quit grilling him?"

"I don't want you to do that for my sake." I finally find my key at the bottom of my bag.

"But I *want* you to come, Maddie."

"Really?" I study his expression, but it's hard to read.

"Yeah. But what if it turns out the old aunt is still living there?" he teases as I unlock the door to my room. "Am I permitted to ask *her* any questions about my dad?"

"Of course," I say as I open the door. "That might actually be interesting."

"Meet you in the lobby," he calls as he goes into his room.

Then I shut the door and stand there for a moment. I think he likes me.

Thirteen

Ian is standing by a very cool sports car that's parked across the street. It's long and low and dark blue.

"That's a Jaguar," observes Ryan as we wave and cross over.

"Expensive?" I ask. I'm sort of oblivious to cars.

"Yeah."

"Ya ready?" Ian asks as he opens the passenger door, nodding to me like I get to sit in front. I glance at Ryan, but he's already getting into the back.

"Cool car," I say to Ian as I slide onto the smooth leather seat.

"Thanks." He grins. "One of the perks of having a somewhat popular eating establishment."

He acts as a tour guide as he drives north, pointing out sites, some I already saw on the bike trip. Ryan is asking good questions and, it seems, keeping his promise not to grill Ian.

It's not long until Ian turns his car onto a gravel road that passes by a few houses clustered together. He says the name of the place, a word I can't even begin to pronounce.

"Mary's cottage is just at the end of this road."

"The aunt?" I ask.

"Yes. Aunt Mary."

I spot a white building up ahead. Shining in the afternoon sun, it has bright blue shutters, a red door, and a thatched roof.

"Is that it?" I ask.

"That's it." Ian parks the car along the road, just a short way from the cottage. "The question is, does she still live here?" He turns around to look at Ryan. "Want me to check first?"

"That's probably a good idea." Ryan's leaning forward to look at the cottage. "Just in case."

After Ian's out of the car, I turn around to see Ryan. His eyes are wide as he stares at the cottage.

"Isn't it pretty?" I say. "Look at those flowering vines growing over the right side of the house. Whoever lives here must have a green thumb."

"It's amazing to think that my ancestors might have lived here," he says. "Or that my father actually came here and stayed here."

"Pretty cool, huh?"

"Yeah, it is."

Ian is talking to a man who looks to be in his thirties. Not a good sign, I'm thinking. And now he's coming back. But he's smiling.

"Mary still lives here," he tells us. "That's her handyman there. He came over to fix a stone fence that's falling down."

"Does she mind if we come in?" Ryan asks as he gets out.

"I'm sure she'll be happy to meet a long-lost relative."

As we walk toward the house, an elderly woman emerges by way of the red door. Her hair is white, but there's a bounce in her step, and a smile breaks across her face as she gets closer. Going straight for Ryan, she walks up and takes him by both hands.

"Mary, I'd like to introduce you to your great-nephew, Ryan McIntire."

"I'd know you anywhere, son. The spitting image of your da, you are. Oh, my Michael would be proud to know you, he would."

Then she hugs him, holding him close for what seems like several minutes but is probably just a few seconds. When she lets go of him and stands there looking at him, I think I see tears in Ryan's eyes. But I'm sure they're happy ones.

Ian continues the introductions, and when I try to call her Miss McIntire, she quickly corrects me. "Just call me Mary, darling," she says as we walk up to the house. The stone walkway is bordered by small flowering plants that look somewhat like primroses. "Some folks even call me Mary Mack, although I'm not terribly fond of that name since I've been hearing that old song since I was a wee one."

She gets a straw sun hat that's hanging on a peg by the front door and proceeds to give us the grand tour of her place, which is like something right out of a picture book or an Irish travel brochure. Not only are her gardens spectacular, but beyond a wall of tall hedges, which she says are to protect the house from the wind, she also has a view of the ocean.

"This is so beautiful," I say as we stand and admire the panorama.

"Our people were fishermen," she says. "Always lived by the sea."

Then she takes us inside. The cottage is bigger than it looks, with lots of small rooms connected to each other. It's filled with antiques and pictures and knickknacks. Really interesting. Finally she invites us to sit in her front room.

"I'll make us tea," she announces.

"Do you need help?" I offer. Wouldn't my mom be proud of me!

"That'd be lovely, dear."

This gives me a chance to check out her adorable little kitchen again. I'm trying to take mental notes, for my mom's sake, since she's really into kitchens, and this one seems like the real Irish deal. I have a camera in my bag, but I don't know if it would be rude to ask to take pictures. I mean, I hardly know this woman.

The kitchen is pretty small, and the floor is covered with tiles that are slightly uneven but thoroughly worn. The walls are painted a bright yellow, about the same color as a dandelion. But you don't see much wall since there are so many things hanging all over the place—pictures, decorative plates, kitchen utensils and pans, as well as a collection of crucifixes that look quite old. I suspect some of these things have been hanging here for generations. There's a large piece of furniture that looks like a dresser against one wall. It's painted a bright blue, the same color as the shutters outside, and topped with colorful ceramic tiles. But this dresser is used for storing dishes, not clothes, because that's where she gets her china teapot and teacups.

"Would you rinse this for me?" she asks as she hands me a delicate teapot. "I only use it for special occasions, and I fear it's covered in dust."

I run hot water over the pretty blue and white piece, careful not to chip it on the old-fashioned faucet. "What is this sink made out of?" I ask when I'm done.

"What's that?" she says, turning to see what I'm talking about. I point to the sink.

"Oh, that. Why, it's soapstone, of course."

"It's made of real stone?"

She smiles. "Aye. Very sturdy, it is."

She's been busy slicing a loaf of bread, along with some other things I'm guessing came from her garden. She now transforms these ingredients into thin sandwiches, which she cuts into dainty triangles. I watch as she arranges these, along with some shortbread cookies from a tin, on a china plate decorated with pink roses.

"Very pretty," I say just as her teakettle begins to whistle.

"You go ahead and take that in," she tells me, "and I'll be along shortly."

I feel like I'm playing a role in an Irish movie classic as I set the plate on the table in the front room.

"Wow," says Ryan. "I thought we were just having tea. This looks more like lunch."

Ian laughs. "This is tea, son."

Now Mary emerges with a tray loaded with her teapot and cups and sugar and cream. I notice that she's removed her apron. She sets the tray down with a flourish and then proceeds to fill our cups, asking us what we'd like in our tea. Finally we're all settled.

"This is really nice," Ryan says to her. "Thanks for going to so much trouble."

"'Tis not trouble, son. 'Tis pure pleasure," she tells him. "I canna tell you how pleased I am to see Michael's boy right here before my eyes. Now, I should be asking you, how are your grandparents? Your grandmother used to write to me occasionally, but after the…" She pauses as if remembering something, which I'm thinking has to do with Ryan's dad. "Well, we simply lost touch, we did."

Ryan fills her in, telling her about his grandfather's death and his grandmother's recent health problems.

"Oh, I'm so sorry to hear of my brother's passing. But not so surprised. I once had five brothers—Frankie, Glen, John, Colin, and Teddy. But now I am all alone. I fear I'm the last of the McIntires in Malin. Most of my nieces and nephews have moved away. Many to the cities, and some have gone off to America." Her eyes get misty. "I fear our family is a thing of the past."

I wonder if this dispersion of relatives is related to Ryan's dad and his involvement in the IRA. Did he bring shame to the family? Or simply sorrow? The room gets quiet for a couple of minutes, uncomfortably quiet, and I desperately try to think of something to say, something to lighten what feels like a blanket of sadness that's fallen on us. Fortunately Ryan beats me to it.

"Ian mentioned how my father used to come to visit you here."

She smiles now. "Aye, he did. When he first came to Ireland, he stayed right here in this very house, he did. Back then I was living here with my sister-in-law Nora. Her husband, my younger brother Teddy, had just died, and Nora and I lived happily here for nearly two decades. But she passed on a couple of years ago. Since then I've lived here alone." She sighs. "I still remember the last time I saw your da, Ryan. Just a day before…"

She sets her teacup down and gets up to go over to the mantel, which is crowded with framed photos that appear to go back several generations. She picks up a small picture in a silver frame and holds it up for us to see. It's a faded color snapshot of a baby. Not a great shot, but at least the baby is smiling brightly.

"Michael gave this to me." She smiles as she adjusts her glasses and studies it more closely. "It's you, Ryan. Michael was so happy that day he was here. He was to fly back home to America the very next day. He told me how much he missed his sweet wife and his baby boy." She hands the photo to Ryan, then reaches into her cardigan pocket to extract a white linen hanky and dab her eyes. "I felt so bad for you and your poor mother, Ryan. So very, very sad, it was."

Ryan nods without speaking.

"Ryan's mother passed away this year," Ian tells Mary, as if he wants to get this other bit of sadness out of the way.

Mary places her hand on Ryan's shoulder and shakes her head. "I'm so sorry, son. It seems you are truly one of the Irish now."

He looks up with a slightly confused expression.

"The sorrows. We Irish seem to have more than our fair share of sorrows."

"Oh."

She takes in a slow, shaky breath, then stands a bit straighter. "We also have more than our fair share of the joys and the blessings. Every day I pray to the blessed Mother Mary to balance these things. And sometimes I think perhaps God, in his wisdom, created the Irish for some divine reason."

Ryan sort of nods. "I'd like to believe that too."

We continue to visit with Mary, and she recalls happier times, sharing stories about Ryan's dad when he stayed with her. "He was quite handy," she says. "The cottage was a wee bit run-down when he came to stay. But he found me da's old tools, and the next thing we knew, he was a-mending things and painting and what have you. 'Twas a real blessing to have him here with us. I think it was during that time that I adopted him into my heart. I came to think of him as my very own."

Ryan smiles. "My mom said my dad loved living in Ireland."

"Aye, he did. He was Irish to the heart." She frowns slightly. "But 'twas a hardship for him too. He was a lot like my brother Colin." She glances at Ian. "You must've met Colin while living in Belfast."

Ian nods without speaking. Something in his expression suggests that Colin isn't someone Ian cares to remember.

"Colin strongly believed in a united Ireland," she continues. "I'm sure he influenced your da, Ryan. 'Twas not my idea for those two to meet. A bit like fire and straw, it was."

"Colin was very involved in the IRA," Ian explains. "Back to the early days of the organization."

"I lay much of the blame for Michael's tragedy upon Colin." She holds her chin up slightly. " 'Twas a sad irony."

"What do you mean?" Ryan asks. "What was a sad irony?"

I'm glad he asks, because this has roused my curiosity as well.

"John, my brother and your grandfather, and Colin bitterly disagreed about certain things. John, being the oldest boy, tried to force young Colin to cease his political involvement, but Colin, being born stubborn, refused. I believe it was one of the main reasons your grandparents left for America when they did, Ryan."

"I didn't know that."

"So you see, these things began long before your father…and they will undoubtedly continue long after we're all gone. Political strife seems to be one of the legacies of the Irish."

Ian is standing now, looking at his watch. "I hate to end this, but I need to be back in Derry by six o'clock for the dinner hour at my restaurant."

Mary stands and clasps Ian's hand in hers. "I thank you for bringing Michael's boy to me, Ian. 'Twas good of ya." Then she turns and wraps her arms around Ryan again. "Please come back and see me if ya can, son."

"I'd like that," he says.

"'Twas a pleasure to meet you as well, Maddie," she tells me with bright, pale blue eyes that appear close to overflowing with tears again. "Ya come back to see me—all of ya—anytime."

We're all fairly quiet as Ian drives us back to the hotel. I'm sure Ryan has a lot to think about and sort through. I know I'm still trying to put some things together. Back in Malin Town, we thank Ian for coming to meet with us and for taking us to see Mary. Just before he gets in the car, he hands me a business card for his restaurant.

"Come in for a meal when you're passing through Derry," he says. "On the house, of course."

"We'll see what we can do," I tell him, although I'm certain there will be snowballs down under before we can convince my aunt to sit down and eat a meal at Ian's restaurant.

Then he looks at Ryan. "I'm sorry I didn't have all the answers you were looking for. But I do believe they will come to you in time. If you keep searching for your own truth, that is."

Ryan looks somewhat puzzled by this. But he nods just the same. "Thanks again," he calls out as Ian waves and pulls away.

"Cool car," I say for the second time as we stand on the sidewalk watching him drive off.

"Interesting day," says Ryan as we walk up the steps to the hotel.

"Don't you think it was weird that Ian never once brought up Sid? Like he never even knew her?"

"Yeah." Ryan holds the door for me. "I almost asked him about her while we were driving up to Malin Head, but I couldn't quite think of how to put it."

"I would've asked him myself," I admit as we walk through the lobby, "except I promised Sid I'd leave her out of this completely."

"Well, you kept your promise."

"Do you think I should tell her about him?"

"I don't know. I mean, what would you say anyway?"

"Not that he *never* mentioned her name. Can you imagine how that would make her feel?"

"Maybe we should keep quiet about the whole thing. At least for the time being. Unless she asks, that is."

"I doubt she'll ask."

As it turns out, she doesn't ask. And we don't tell. But as we drive through Derry the following morning on our way to Belfast, I glance at the street names and wonder where a particular restaurant might be located. I suspect Ryan might be doing the same. Even so, neither of us mentions it or anything else to do with Ian McMahan. Like my dad would say, let sleeping dogs lie.

To my relief, Sid is acting pretty much like her old self as she drives toward Belfast. It turns out that yesterday's interview went well for her, and as a result her article on the peace camp is almost done. But the way she keeps chattering, maintaining this overly cheerful attitude, makes me think all this might be a cover-up. It could be her way of pretending that our meeting with Ian meant nothing to her. It could mean that she's really hurting inside.

"I can't believe we're really in Northern Ireland," she says as we drive through countryside that looks no different from any of the other Irish countryside. Just as pretty and green and scenic as the rest of the island.

"Why's that?" I ask as I absently gaze out the window, looking at the familiar black-faced sheep that seem to be everywhere.

"The last time I was here, back in the dark ages—otherwise known as the seventies—you would get stopped before going across the border. You had to show your passport and go through a checkpoint just to get in. There were British armed forces and guns and the works. Just like a war zone. It was pretty unsettling, really. Now you just drive across. No big deal. You'd hardly know you'd crossed a border."

"Isn't that a good thing?" Ryan asks.

"Of course. It just feels so different."

"Maybe the whole peace agreement and the disarmament thing is working," I say.

"In some respects. But don't forget about last week's bombing," she says, "and the RIRA."

"How many members are in the RIRA?" I ask.

"Hopefully not many."

Belfast turns out to be a very large city, and I'm impressed with how much Sid's driving skills have improved, because the traffic here is gnarly. Sid drives around, pointing out some of the sights like Queen's University, Belfast Castle, the parliament buildings, and several beautiful cathedrals. We finally wind up in a hotel right in the middle of the city.

"I'm going to be busy doing research and writing for the next couple of days," she explains as we load our baggage onto a big brass cart in the underground parking lot. "I figured this downtown location would be fun for you two. You can book tours through the hotel or just wander around the city and discover things for yourself."

"Sounds great," I tell her as we walk toward the elevators.

I think I'm relieved that she has work to do. All day long I've been feeling guilty about our meeting with Ian yesterday—like Sid was left out in the cold, and suffering as a result. All her cheerful chatter and upbeat attitude, which just barely ring false, are starting to bug me. A couple of days might be what we need to put the whole Ian thing behind us. Poor Sid.

fourteen

R yan and I begin our first day in Belfast by grabbing a quick breakfast at the McDonald's that's just a block away from our hotel. Okay, I know American fast food is a huge cop-out, but this enables us to catch the nine o'clock open-bus tour. The open bus is a big red double-decker deal with an open place to sit on top. Okay, it's a little unsettling, since I've heard of bombs going off in these. But that was most recently in London and not even related to the RIRA. And I seriously doubt it will happen here today.

The tour takes about an hour and gives us a bit more of an overview of the city than what Sid gave us yesterday. But afterward I want to get a better look at Belfast Castle, and Ryan wants to look at the shipyards. He informs me that the *Titanic* was made here.

"The movie?" I say, instantly realizing how stupid that sounds.

But he just laughs. "They had to make the boat first, Maddie. The movie came later."

So we part ways. And I have to say I'm relieved to have some time to myself today. The past few days have been jam-packed and somewhat stressful for me. I mean, it's been really interesting too, but I'm ready for a mental-health break. I also noticed there are some pretty cool shopping places around here, and I want to find a few things to impress my friends when I get home. Katie brought home all kinds of cool stuff from their trip to Europe last year. Thinking of Katie makes me wonder if she's gotten engaged yet. I hope not. Even though I'm feeling more grown-up now, a lot older than when I left for this trip just a week and a half ago, I still think nineteen is way too young to get engaged. I'm halfway tempted to break Dad's cell-phone rule (emergencies only) and give her a call, along with a piece of my mind.

I feel a small wave of homesickness as I stand on the corner, waiting for the bus that the hotel concierge said will take me to the castle. I've only been homesick a couple of times so far, and it hasn't lasted long. But the way I feel right now takes me by surprise. I suddenly miss my parents and my brother and the farm and my friends and everything. I remind myself that I'll be back home in five days. And then, still feeling a little blue, I actually take a moment to pray for them. I even thank God for them. Compared to Ryan and Sid, I have it pretty good when it comes to family. I guess it's something I've always taken for granted.

The city bus arrives, and I get on with several others. As the bus makes a turn, a street sign catches my attention. Antrim Street? Now why is that name familiar? Then I remember that Antrim was the place Ian mentioned the other day—the place he drove to instead of taking Ryan's dad to the airport. I decide to pull out my map of Ireland and find out where Antrim actually is. After searching a while, I realize that Antrim is actually the name of the county where Belfast is located. But then I see it's also a town, and it's only a little ways north of Belfast—in fact, it's not very far from the airport. This makes me wonder why Ian wasn't able to do his errand and also go to the airport. Why didn't he just take Ryan's dad with him to Antrim? Maybe it was Ian's excuse to part ways with Michael. But why? Michael was leaving the country anyway. What difference could a few more hours make? Of course, those hours would've cost Ian his life. I feel like a dog chasing its tail as I run these facts around in my head.

The more I think about it and the more I study these places on my map, the more I wonder if Ian was telling us the truth after all. I remember how Ryan kept questioning him about these things, and I think I'm beginning to see why Ryan thought Ian's story was a little fishy. A little too convenient. Although I must admit that I found Ian's story quite believable, at the time anyway. On the other hand, I can be pretty gullible. The old fresh-off-the-farm thing isn't too far from the truth.

Just as the bus stops to let us out near the castle, which actually looks fairly spectacular, I remind myself I was not going to think about this stressful stuff anymore. Today is supposed to be *my* day, my chance to just relax and enjoy Belfast and shopping and whatever trips my trigger. And that's what I intend to do. I will put all thoughts of Ian, along with the whole confusing IRA business, totally out of my head.

Touring the castle is a good distraction. It's really quite beautiful, although it's not as old as I'd thought. The original castle was built in the twelfth century, but the current one came several replacement castles later and is only about one hundred fifty years old or so. I have to laugh to myself about this. Where I live, the only things older than that would be the Lewis and Clark trail and, of course, the Native Americans' history. In comparison, this is pretty old.

The view from the castle is excellent. It's situated on a hill called Cave Hill, which has a history all its own. But you can see most of Belfast from up here. And the gardens and grounds are spectacular.

After walking around for a couple of hours, my right sandal starts to give me a blister on my big toe, and I decide to treat myself to lunch in the restaurant that's located in the cellar. I feel kind of silly at first, eating alone where there are mostly groups or families or couples. Then I remind myself that I'm actually in a castle in Ireland! And I take some time to write some postcards, as well as in my journal, and I try to act as if this is no big deal, like I do things like this every day. Yeah, right.

I'm not that surprised when my food comes and it is excellent. The Irish really know how to eat!

After that, I catch the bus to a shopping district we passed on the way. While most of the stores are out of my price range, I manage to find one store with some pretty cool stuff that's not horribly expensive. I really feel like I need to get something that I can show off to Katie. Not that she'll be impressed since she's probably busy planning her wedding by now. Although I hope not!

By four o'clock I'm feeling beat. I get back on the city bus and, due to daydreaming about how cool I'll look in the outfit I just bought, I end up missing the stop by my hotel. After riding for what seems too long, I finally ask the driver, and he tells me that it's quite a ways back there, but if I stay on the bus and go all the way through his route, which means going up to the castle again, I will eventually get back to my hotel. Or I can get out and walk the twelve or so blocks or try to get a taxi. Due to my now-throbbing toe, I decide to just keep riding. It's about five thirty by the time I finally get off at my hotel. Oh well.

I go to the room I'm sharing with Sid, and it doesn't look like she's back yet. So I soak my hot feet in cold water and then take a little nap. My aunt didn't say for sure when she'd be back, and when I notice it's nearly seven and she's still not here, I realize I'm getting hungry for dinner. But the idea of eating another meal by myself isn't too appealing. I call Ryan's room, but he doesn't seem to be in either. I consider calling down for room service, but I've heard that's really expensive.

Instead, I get dressed in the new outfit, which makes me look like I'm in my twenties, and I leave my aunt a note. Then I head downstairs, where I ask the concierge if there are any good places to eat nearby. She tells me of several within walking distance, including a nearby pub with a weird name. "But it's quite popular with people your age," she says with a smile.

"Can you repeat that name again?" I say, unsure of what she just said.

"Ádh Mór!" she says slowly. "How about if I write it down for you?"

So now I have the name of this pub and am standing in the lobby considering my options when I see Ryan coming in. "Hey, Ryan," I call out as I hurry over to him. I can't believe how thankful

I am to see a familiar face just now. It's like I was starting to feel as though I'd been abandoned in Ireland.

"Maddie," he says as he comes over. "Fancy meeting you here."

"Yeah, right." I give him my *duh* look. "I was just about to get something to eat."

"Where's Sid?"

"She's not back yet."

"Want any company?" he asks.

"Sure," I say in a tone that doesn't convey how bad I want some company. Then I tell him about the popular pub and show him what the concierge wrote down for me.

He laughs. "You've changed a lot in the past week. Remember how you threw a fit when we ate in pubs?"

"Well, I understand that it's *different* here in Ireland," I remind him. "Do you need anything in your room before we go?"

He looks down at his T-shirt and jeans and then back at me. "I don't know, Maddie. You look pretty hot. Do I look good enough to be seen with you?"

I laugh, but I don't miss the compliment as I tug at his arm. "You look fine, Ryan. But I'm hungry. Let's go."

"Should we leave Sid a message about where we've gone?"

I consider this. "I left her a note that I was going out for a bite. Maybe that's enough. I have a feeling she needs some space right now. You know?"

He nods as we head out onto the street. "Yeah, I thought that same thing today. Do you think she's still feeling bad about Ian?"

"I'd be surprised if she wasn't." Then I point to the left. "The concierge said this way. It's about two blocks down on the same side of the street." Then I ask him about the shipyard and tell him about the castle. It seems we both had a good day.

"Here we are," I say as I point to the sign.

The pub is noisy and pretty full when we go inside. But we manage to get a table close to the band, which is just starting to set up. I'm guessing it'll be loud right here, but at least we get to hear live music.

"I was playing my drum last night," Ryan says. "Could you guys hear me?"

"No."

"Good, I was afraid someone might call down and complain."

"You said you played guitar and bass," I say now. "How long have you played?"

"Since I was about fifteen. I was in a band for a few years, but we kind of fell apart when we went to college. We still get together to jam sometimes."

"I was in a band too."

"No way."

I laugh. "Yeah. It wasn't much of a band, but we had fun."

"A girls' band?"

"No, we had guys too."

"And you said you played guitar too?"

"Yeah. I haven't played much this past year. But playing around with my penny whistle makes me want to get back into music."

He nods. "I was thinking the same thing. I was wishing I could jam with some people who know a little about Irish music."

I glance over to where the amplifiers are getting set up. "I don't think that's what we'll be hearing tonight."

We talk more about music as well as other things more pertinent to our lives back home, and it occurs to me that our friendship seems to be going to a deeper level. I also remember that he said I looked hot tonight. I can't help but wonder what it would be like to be involved with someone like Ryan. I mean, he's a great guy, and he's even a Christian. Why wouldn't I think about it?

Just as we're finishing our dinners, the band starts to play. And, man, are they loud! I seriously consider sticking my fingers in my ears, but I don't want to look that stupid. Fortunately, it seems Ryan has read my expression, because after just one song, he suggests we get out of here.

"Thanks," I tell him when we're finally outside and I can hear again.

"That sound system was pretty bad."

"Not to mention loud," I reply.

Then we just walk along without saying much for about a block. We're going in the direction of the hotel, but I'm not really ready to call it a night. And yet I can't think of anything to suggest.

"Want to find a quieter place?" he asks. "We could get some coffee or dessert or something."

"Sounds good."

Then Ryan spots a coffee shop across the street and several doors down. It appears to be open, so we head that way and are relieved to find that, other than some jazz music playing on their sound system, it is relatively quiet in there.

We both order coffee and sit down. But suddenly I feel sort of awkward. It's that old feeling, like, is this a date? Or are we just two travelers who got stuck together by my aunt, and he's simply putting up with me? Oh, maybe it doesn't even matter.

"I didn't tell you this," he says as he stirs the cream into his coffee, "but the other day when we drove out to Malin Head, well, I was relieved you came with me. I think it helped to make things easier, you know."

"Hey, I had a good time. I think your aunt is awesome."

"It was cool getting to know her, seeing her place…"

"So are you feeling better, you know, about things with your dad?" I hope I'm not being too intrusive, but I am curious.

He shrugs. "It's still hard to understand, but I guess it's getting easier. It's kind of like Ian said, I sort of have to piece things together for myself."

For some reason this reminds me of Antrim—a puzzle piece I don't quite get. And before I know it, I've told him.

He frowns. "Really?"

"Yeah. I probably shouldn't have mentioned it. But it was weird seeing that sign on the way to the castle. I mean, it's not like I really cared where Antrim was located before. But for some reason, it caught my attention, and then when I found it on my map, well, I was surprised at how close it was to Belfast."

"That does seem strange."

"And it's pretty close to the airport too."

Ryan seems frustrated by this. And now I feel even worse for having brought it up. Maybe we all just need to move on.

"I'm sure there's some logical explanation," I say, hoping to brush this all away.

"Do you still have Ian's business card?"

I nod.

"Maybe I'll give him a call before we leave Ireland. Just to ask, you know. It'd be easier to do it before I get back home."

"Yeah, I guess." I study his troubled expression and want to kick myself for having mentioned Antrim. We were having this good time, and I was actually feeling like we were getting closer. And now he's all focused on his dad again, looking for answers where there might not be any. When will I learn?

Fifteen

"Want to take a black-taxi tour today?" Sid asks us at breakfast. It's our last day in Belfast, and she's almost done with her peace-camp research and, as a result, seems in a pretty good mood.

"What's that?" I ask as I butter my toast.

"It's a tour of West Belfast," she tells me.

"And?" I still don't get it.

"It's where the troubles took place," Ryan fills in.

"How come you always know so much?" I tease him.

"I've done my research." He turns to Sid. "And I'd really like to see it. I heard you can even get a glimpse of the Sinn Féin headquarters."

"What does that mean?" I ask. "Sinn Féin? I've heard it before. Is it the name of someone?"

"It means 'ourselves,'" my aunt informs me.

"It's about Irish self-rule," Ryan continues. "In the early part of the twentieth century, there was this huge turnover in the Irish parliament. I think it was about 1918 or so. But Irishmen were elected to the majority of parliament seats, booting out the British loyalists. And then the new Irish representatives refused to meet in England. They insisted on Dublin instead. And as a result, things got sticky."

"That was the official beginning of the IRA," my aunt finishes for him.

"Thanks for the history lesson," I tell them. Actually, I'm glad to know this. It helps me to understand this country a little better.

"So you up for a black-taxi tour, then?"

"Sounds good to me."

We check out of our hotel and put our bags in the car. And at ten o'clock the taxi arrives and takes us into West Belfast.

"This is Falls Road," the driver tells us. "Mostly Catholic republicans live here." Then he points out the Sinn Féin headquarters, and Ryan leans out the window to get a shot.

"They're really into graffiti here," I observe.

"We prefer to think of it as art," he tells me.

I notice strings of fluttering flags along the roadside. "What's that?" I ask.

"Them's the Easter lilies," says the driver.

"Easter lilies?" I'm confused. For one thing, they look nothing like lilies, and besides that, it's June.

"To remind us of them that died in the Easter Rising back in 1916, as well as for them that's died since."

"The Easter Rising preceded the Irish War of Independence," Ryan adds.

"Tha's right." The driver nods vigorously, as if he's impressed with Ryan's grasp of Irish history. I know I am.

The driver points out more things, explaining some of the meaning behind the graffiti art. "That one there's for the H-Block Martyrs," he says as he points to a large and well-done mural.

Okay, I'm thinking, does he mean H&R Block? And what does that have to do with Ireland?

"Bobby Sands," my aunt says.

"Tha's right." The driver nods again. "Him's the inspiration behind it all."

Ryan looks at me and grins. "You have confusion written all over your face, Maddie."

I kind of shrug.

"Bobby Sands went on a hunger strike," Sid explains, "and some fellow IRA inmates followed suit."

"And died," adds Ryan.

"They starved themselves to death?" I ask.

"Tha's right." The driver slows down and points to what appears to be a cemetery. "Most of 'em are buried there. Tha's Milltown Cemetery."

He parks nearby, and we all sit in the taxi and just look.

"Now would you like to see the other side o' things?"

"Sure," my aunt tells him.

He drives on until we come to some sort of an entrance. There are tall gates painted red and white, and he drives through.

"Welcome to Shankill Road," he tells us.

"This is the Protestant side," Sid adds.

We drive alongside a tall, imposing wall that seems to slice through the neighborhoods like a knife. It appears to be made of concrete blocks, and the bottom part is painted white and covered with all sorts of graffiti. I notice that the houses on the other side, the Catholic side, are crowded together and sit very close to the wall, whereas this side, the Protestant side, seems much more open, and the houses are situated a comfortable distance from the wall. I wonder why that is.

"Tha's the peace wall," the driver says, pointing to the ominous barrier. "Put there to keep the Catholics and the Protestants from killing each other."

He slows down so we can actually look out the window and read the graffiti. Soon we are reading slogans out loud to each other.

"Be the solution you want to see in the world," Sid reads. "Gandhi."

"How about this?" I say. "So many tears, too many years, no more spilled blood, let's learn to love."

"That's nice," my aunt says.

"Here's a good one," says Ryan. "You all believe in the same God, so listen to him."

"Amen," I add to this. And Sid echoes my sentiment.

Then the driver shows us places where we can see traces of bombings, and Sid takes photos.

"Some thought we were done with all that," he says as he drives us back toward the city. "But last week we had another."

"The Orange Rose?" says Sid.

"Aye. Nasty bit o' business, that was."

"Can you drive us by?" she asks. "To get some photos?"

"I'm not sure I can get through there," he says. "The street was blocked off just a couple of days ago."

"I'm a journalist," she tells him. "It's for a story."

He nods. "We'll see what we can do."

As it turns out, the street is no longer blocked, and he slowly drives past a brick building with sheets of plywood covering what must've been blown-out windows. Sid snaps a number of photos.

"Too bad," she says as she leans back into the seat.

"Do you think this will ever end?" Ryan asks the driver. "Is there any chance for peace here?"

"Not unless all the loyalists pick up and leave," he says. "And that's not likely to happen."

"I'm guessing you're Catholic," Ryan ventures.

The driver nods. "But I believe in peace." He reaches for a photo of three young children that's attached by a magnet to his dashboard and holds it up for us to see. "I grew up during the troubles, and I don't want my family to go through that."

"I don't blame you," my aunt tells him as she looks at the photo. "Cute kids."

"Thanks." He puts the photo back.

"Have you heard much about this new IRA?" she asks. "What they're calling the *Real* IRA?"

"Aye. Everyone's heard o' them."

"What do you think of their organization?"

He shakes his head with a frown. "No' so much."

"Do you think they're serious?"

"You saw the Orange Rose," he reminds her.

"Do you think they're a very large organization?"

He seems to consider this. "I hope not. But I fear what they lack in numbers they will make up for in violence."

"Oh." I can see her making a mental note of this comment.

"And I hear they are a vengeful lot."

"How's that?" my aunt persists.

"There's an old Irish saying that suits them to a *T,*" he says. "For every Irishman on the fire, there will always be another ready to turn the spit."

"What's that mean?" asks Ryan.

"In the case of the Real IRA, it means they will turn on their own if their own turn away from the cause."

Sid actually digs in her bag for her notebook now and quickly writes these things down.

Before long, our tour ends, and we're back at our hotel. Sid gives the driver a generous tip, and we all thank him for the informative tour.

"We have time to get some lunch before we head out," Sid tells us. "How about something within walking distance?"

Ryan and I tell her about the pub we visited last night. "The food was great," he says, "but the music was really loud."

"They probably wouldn't have music in the daytime," I say. And so we decide to head back to the Ádh Mór!

"What does *ádh mór* mean?" I ask the waitress when she comes to take our order.

First she corrects my pronunciation. Then she tells me it means "good luck" or "cheers."

"Kind of like that old TV sitcom," Sid says.

The waitress nods, then actually sings a line from the theme song. "Sometimes you wanna go where everybody knows your name."

We laugh and even clap for her. Then she takes a bow, along with our order.

"So you favor the Catholic pubs in Belfast?" my aunt teases Ryan.

"How do you know it's Catholic?" I ask.

"It's just a guess. But establishments that use the Irish language are often republican and often Catholic." She points to a green banner. "And that's a pretty good clue."

"What?" I ask.

"The color green. It usually stands for Irish republicans. And orange is for national loyalists."

"Is that why the Protestant pub was called the Orange Rose?"

She nods, then frowns. "Sometimes I just get so angry at all this."

"All this what?" I ask.

"Division. Strife. Violence. Hatred." She shakes her head in disgust. "I've never particularly cared for the IRA or their methods."

"You and my mom both," Ryan says with a bit of impatience.

"It's cost your family a lot," she reminds him. "And lots of other people even more."

"But you've got to see why they did it," he tells her. "You've got to understand where they were coming from."

"Maybe. Or maybe I thought I did. But I'm not so sure anymore. And to think that the RIRA is the offspring of the old IRA." She lets out a long, jagged sigh. "Well, it just makes me sick."

"They're not the same organization," he says. "The original IRA has agreed to the peace talks and the disarmament."

"So they say."

"You don't believe them?"

"I don't know. But I'm finding that the older I get, the less tolerant I am for violent activities of any kind."

"Our country has some pretty violent roots, if you think about our own fight for independence," Ryan reminds her.

"Yes, yes…I'm well aware of that. And in some ways our situation wasn't much different from here."

"Bloodier," he says. "And what about the Civil War? That's similar too."

"I know, I know." She rolls her eyes. "I guess I'm just saying I hate war and violence in general. Okay?"

"I know what you mean," I agree. "It was so sad seeing West Belfast literally split in half by that ugly wall."

"I keep thinking of that quote I read on the peace wall today," Ryan says, "about believing in the same God but not listening to him. I think that might be a universal problem."

Sixteen

"We have just enough time to make it to the peace camp for my appointment," Sid tells us as we're finishing lunch.

"When's your appointment?" I ask before drinking the last of my lemon soda.

"Three." She signs the receipt for her Visa card.

"But it's already after two," Ryan points out.

"We're fine," she assures him.

It takes about fifteen minutes to get outside of the city, and then Sid heads north on the highway. After about twenty minutes of driving, she slows down and exits the highway. I notice that the sign where she turns off says Antrim, and I can't help but reach from the backseat to nudge Ryan. He nods back at me as if he, too, has noticed.

"Where is the camp?" I ask.

"It's just north of Antrim. As I told you, it's on an estate that was donated by a wealthy family back in the early seventies. The wife was Catholic and the husband Protestant."

"That explains a lot," I say.

"It's a beautiful setting," she continues as she slowly drives through the town of Antrim. "Located right on the lake so there's swimming and boating and fishing."

"Is that Lough Neagh?" I ask as I locate the lake on my map.

"That's right. It's the largest lake in Ireland."

"It's handy that the camp is so close to Belfast," Ryan comments. "A short commute for the campers."

"Yes," she agrees as she turns down a narrow road. "And yet it's like a totally different world up here. A real escape for the children."

It's not quite three when Sid parks in front of what appears to be a small castle. The sign above the oversized, carved wooden front door reads Peace House.

"This is it," she says happily. "You guys feel free to look around while I go in to talk to the camp director."

So we wander around the gardens surrounding the large stone structure. It seems fairly quiet and not exactly what you'd expect to find in a youth camp. But as we get closer to the lake, we begin to hear voices. And eventually we come across a playing field and some small stone cottages that I'm guessing are used to house the campers. When we reach the lakeside, with its docks and boats, we find kids all over the place.

"Now this looks more like summer camp," I say to Ryan.

"Can I help you?" a tall, red-headed guy with a clipboard asks us. Judging by his accent, he's not Irish. I'm guessing he's an American.

So we explain why we're here, and he suggests we go back to check in with the main office inside Peace House.

"It's for security reasons," he explains. "Glenda will take your information and give you nametags, which work as security passes."

"No problem," Ryan tells him, and we head back.

"Can't really blame them for that," I say as we walk across the big green lawn again.

"I guess. But who would want to hurt these little kids?" he asks. "I mean, they're Catholic *and* Protestant, from both sides of the wall."

"Remember what the taxi driver told us," I remind him, "about how the RIRA will turn on their own."

He nods. "Maybe. But it just doesn't make sense."

I want to say *duh* but restrain myself.

So we meet Glenda, the office lady, and tell her who we are and then fill out some forms. She gives us our nametags as well as a map of the estate.

"Enjoy your visit at Peace House." She nods to the large lobby outside the office. "And you can look around inside as well. Just don't go into any of the rooms marked Private."

So we decide to explore the interior of Peace House, and although it's obvious this place was once quite swanky, it's fairly plain now. Other than some elegant chandeliers and a few carpets and paintings, it's mostly furnished with institutional types of furniture.

"I wonder if the kids can slide down this banister," I say as I rub my hand along its polished marble finish.

"I don't think you should try it," Ryan warns me.

We reach the top of the stairs and find that most of the rooms are private.

"Want to go up to the next floor?" I ask when I spot a smaller staircase at the end of the hallway.

"Sure, why not?" he says. "Might be a good view of the lake up there."

Here we discover a large room that perhaps was once a ballroom. But now it appears to be an activity room with lots of tables and arts-and-crafts supplies. Then we go down another hallway that opens up to a round room with windows around nearly three-fourths of it.

"Check out the view," I say as I go over to the windows and look out to see the bright blue lake surrounded by green grass and trees. "Wow."

All along the bottoms of these tall windows are benches with cushions. "This has to be the biggest window seat I've ever seen," I tell Ryan as I sit down and look around. "Awesome!"

Now I notice that the one section of wall without windows is full of bookshelves, and there are comfortable-looking chairs as well as oversized pillows and rugs all around the room. "This must be a reading room," I say.

"I guess they need something for the rainy days here," says Ryan as we both sit on the window seat and gaze out at the lake below us.

"It's so cool that someone donated this place for a peace camp," I say. "No wonder Sid and Danielle loved being here."

"Yeah." He nods, but he has a faraway look in his eyes. Like I'm not even here with him.

I'm guessing he's thinking about his mom. Maybe even trying to imagine how it was when his parents were here so many years ago. For that reason I just sit quietly, not wanting to intrude on his space. We sit there for several minutes. Then Ryan seems to snap out of it.

"Sorry," he says as he quickly stands. "I guess I was kind of zoned out."

"It's okay."

"It's really nice here."

We walk around the perimeter of the room and stop to look at a section of wall beside the bookshelves that has old photos hanging on it. Most are black-and-white group shots of young people. I'm guessing volunteer counselors.

"Look at this," Ryan says with excitement as he points to one with "1975" on it. "This is when Mom and Sid were here."

We both peer at the slightly fuzzy photo, and finally I think I spot my aunt. "Look," I tell him. "That's Sid."

He looks more closely. "And that's my mom on her right."

I stare at these two girls, just a year or two older than I am, and I think how cool it was for them to give up a summer to volunteer here.

"Your mom was cute," I tell Ryan.

He nods.

"You look a lot like her."

He turns and smiles at me. "You think so?"

Now I'm kind of embarrassed. But I say yes and pretend to refocus on the photos.

We stand there for a while longer, and I'm a little uncomfortable, staring at a bunch of photos of people I don't even know. Then something catches my eye.

"Look at this," I say as I point to the photo that interests me. "This one was taken a few years after the one with Sid and Danielle. But wait. Don't you think that could be Ian?"

I point to the tall guy standing in the middle of the back row.

"Maybe," he says as he studies the shot.

"I mean, he's obviously a lot younger, but look at those eyes, that chin. Don't you think it could be him?"

Ryan points out a tall, dark-haired guy in another group shot, taken a few years later, that looks even more like Ian.

Ryan points at the date now. "Hey, that's the year I was born," he says slowly. "The same year my dad died."

"Oh."

"That's so weird."

"Do you think Ian was involved in the peace camp?" I ask.

He just shrugs. "I have no idea, Maddie."

"But look at that guy," I persist. "Seriously, doesn't he look just like Ian?"

"I'm not sure."

"I'm going to find out about this," I say with a determination that surprises even me.

"How?"

"Maybe I'll ask Glenda in the office," I say. "She looks old enough to have been here awhile."

I practically run down the stairs now, avoiding the temptation to slide down the marble banister. Ryan is just a few steps behind me.

"Excuse me," I say as I burst into her office.

She looks up at me and blinks. "Is anything wrong, dear?"

"No. But I'm wondering about the history of the camp," I tell her. "Is there a way to find out the names of people who have volunteered here over the years?"

She considers this.

"Or perhaps you know," I suggest. "Have you worked here long?"

"Just since I retired from teaching," she says. "That's been about five years."

"Oh."

"There are some old photo albums in the back room. I've been trying to get someone to organize them." She shakes her head as she stands. "They're quite dusty and messy, but they do have some names and such written in them. I think someone should rescue them before it's too late."

"Would you mind if we looked at them?"

She looks unsure now, as if she may not completely trust us.

"We'll be very careful," I promise.

"I'm sure you would be, dear, but I'm a bit worried. If something should happen or if something was lost…" She scratches her head as if trying to come up with a solution. "I know!" She smiles now. "Perhaps Murphy can help you."

"Murphy?"

"Our primary groundskeeper. He's been here for ages, he has. And a memory like an elephant. Murphy might know who you're looking for."

"Do you know where we could find him?" I ask.

She glances at the clock on the wall, then pulls out a map of the estate. Taking a highlighter, she marks a bright yellow trail to a cottage that appears to be on the edge of the property. "He'll probably be taking his tea 'bout now."

"We don't want to disturb—"

"No, no," she waves her hand. "Murphy loves company, he does. And he loves the chance to talk." She laughs. "Just don't let him talk the legs off of you."

So I thank her, and we go back outside.

"Do you want to come with me?" I ask Ryan. He's been pretty quiet since I got stuck on this Ian-at-peace-camp thing, and I'm a little worried that he thinks I've gone off the deep end.

"I don't know, Maddie."

I nod. "I'm sure it sounds pretty crazy. And I could be totally wrong. But for some reason I need to check this out."

He glances over his shoulder toward the lake.

"And if you'd rather hang out by the water or take a boat out or whatever"—I force a smile—"I won't blame you at all."

"Maybe I'll do that."

"Sure, that's fine." Okay, the truth is, I'm feeling a little abandoned just now. I'm remembering how he appreciated me going to meet his Aunt Mary. I would think he'd want to do as much for me.

"Sitting and listening to some old dude going on about people I don't even know…" He kind of shrugs. "Well, I guess I'm just not that into it."

"I understand." But I think he just doesn't want to know the truth about what Ian might have been doing here. Maybe it would hurt too much. I start to walk away now.

"But I could go," he calls out, "if you really want me to…"

"It's okay, Ryan," I call back. "I'll catch up with you later."

"Good luck," he says.

Yeah, I'm thinking as I walk away, *I'll probably need it.* I mean, seriously, what am I thinking? I've barely even met Ian, and the photo I saw just now was taken more than twenty years ago and isn't even that clear. What on earth makes me so sure it's Ian? And yet, it's like I can't leave without finding out. And I'm surprised Ryan isn't more curious.

I follow the bright yellow highlighted trail on my map until I finally see a little stone cottage that, unlike the campers' cottages, actually looks like it was built a long time ago. Like maybe hundreds of years ago. The enormous oak trees hovering around it look like they've been here that long too. Suddenly I'm wondering whether I can just walk up and knock on a stranger's door and interrupt his teatime to ask him a totally stupid question. What was I thinking? And what if Glenda is really a prankster in disguise and has it out for this Murphy fellow? Or what if this Murphy fellow is some kind of nutcase or sex offender? Of course, they wouldn't let someone like that work at a kids' camp, would they?

I'm about twenty feet from the cottage now, standing in the shadows of the enormous trees, just about ready to turn and run.

"Are you lost?" calls a voice from the cottage.

I peer into the shadows to see the face of an old man peeking out from the half-opened door.

"I'm sorry," I say.

He opens the door wider. "Have you lost your way, dear?"

"No." I hold up the map as if that explains everything. "Glenda told me that a man named Murphy lives here."

He smiles now and steps out so I can see him better. "That'd be me." He's wearing brown trousers topped with a dark green vest. And his face looks friendly.

"I don't want to disturb you," I say, "but Glenda said you wouldn't mind if I asked you some questions."

"Come in, come in," he says, opening the door fully and waving me inside. "I'm just having me tea. Come in and join me."

Okay, I'm not so sure I want to step into this strange man's cottage. I mean, he seems nice enough, but this is so weird. And the setting reminds me of a scene from "Hansel and Gretel." What if he has a big wooden stove in there for cooking children? Or perhaps a cage? Okay, I tell myself, don't be ridiculous. This little old man is several inches shorter than me, and he looks to be about eighty. Surely I could take him if I had to.

I walk up to the door and glance inside. Everything looks per-

fectly normal. He has a small wooden table that does appear to be
set for tea, and he's already rounding up another cup and saucer, I
assume for me.

"Sorry I didn't tidy up," he says as he picks a newspaper off a
chair and scoots it up to the table for me. "I didn't know I was having company."

A small brown dog comes bouncing toward me. He puts both
paws on my legs and looks up with his pink tongue hanging off to
one side.

"Oh, now, Lucy, let's leave our visitor be." He nods to me. "Sit
down, sit down."

So I sit down and pet the dog, which makes me feel a little better. An old man with a dog—how dangerous could he be? And
now he's pouring my tea and asking what I take in it.

"Just sugar," I tell him.

He hands it to me. "So, what brings you my way?" He pauses,
and I realize he doesn't even know my name.

"I'm sorry," I say quickly. "I'm Maddie. Madison Chase. I'm
from America."

He smiles. "I knew you weren't from these parts, lassie. But then
we get lots of young people from all over the world here."

"Yes," I say as I pick up my cup. "And that's why I'm here. I
mean, I'm not here as a volunteer. I came with my aunt. She worked
here back in the seventies."

He nods. "In the seventies. That's when we started this camp."

"So you were here then?"

"I was here even before then." He winks at me. "I came with

the place. I've been keeping the grounds since 1942. And even then we were taking in the wee ones."

"What?" I look curiously at him.

"During the war, lassie. Children from London were sent here to escape the bombings and such." He sighs now. "And then they came here again during the troubles. Also to escape the bombings and such."

"This place has quite a history."

"Aye, it does."

"And Glenda said you have quite a memory."

"Tha's true as well."

But even as I prepare to ask my next question, I wonder how it's possible for him to remember everyone who ever volunteered here. So I decide to start with my aunt. I tell him her name and wait to see if it rings a bell.

He just shakes his head. "Sorry, lassie. I canna recall her."

So I tell him about Danielle, and his eyes light up. "Aye, I remember that one. And now that I think of it, I remember her friend too. Pretty lasses, they were. And as I recall, Danielle had a suitor." Now his face grows sad. "Aye, I remember now. The Irish lad from America. Joined up with the IRA. Sad story, that one."

I nod. "Yes. Their son, Ryan, is here with my aunt and me. That's one of the reasons I'm trying to find out about another man." I pause. "Do you recall a man named Ian McMahan ever being here?"

He smiles now. "Ian?"

"Yes."

Then he rubs his hand across his mouth as if he doesn't want to answer me. "I don't know, lassie."

"But it seemed like you knew him," I persist. "And I'm sure I saw his photo in the reading room. Has Ian worked here?"

He sighs. "I'm not sure."

"Do you know someone named Ian McMahan?"

He considers this. "May I ask why it is you're asking about this Ian McMahan person?"

So I tell him about my aunt and her broken heart and how Ian had a connection with Ryan's dad. And I can tell by his expression he knows all about that. What I don't get is why he's not telling me anything.

"You do know who I'm talking about," I say finally. "Don't you?"

But he still doesn't say anything. And I have a feeling I'm wearing out my welcome. But I'm also getting irritated. So I decide to get my biggest question out on the table.

"Okay," I begin. "For some reason you aren't going to tell me about Ian. But I'm going to ask you one more thing: It's really bothering Ryan and me, thinking that Ian might still be in the IRA. I mean, he claims he's not. But some things just don't make sense. Do you know if he's in the IRA?"

Talk about stepping over a line! I'm sure I've gone way too far. Poor old Murphy is sitting there staring at me like I popped down from another planet and threatened to take his little dog hostage.

"I'm sorry for troubling you," I say. I stand up and thank him for the tea I've barely touched and then walk out. But I'm so frustrated that I just stand outside his door with my fists clenched. *Why is he being so tight-lipped about this?*

Then I feel a hand on my shoulder, and it makes me nearly jump out of my sandals.

"Sorry, lassie." He steps around so I can see him better, and then he peers into my eyes as if trying to see something in there. "I'm trying to know if I can trust you or not, and I'm thinking perhaps I can. Would you care to come back inside and finish your tea?"

I mutely follow him back into his little house, sit down again at the table, and wait.

"Whatever I tell you today," he begins, "I tell you in confidence. Can I trust you to keep this confidence?"

"Yes."

"Ian is a friend of mine," he says. "And it's not so much that he has asked me to remain silent on his account. But I do worry for the boy. He has old connections, connections he has worked to sever, but connections that remain, just the same."

"To the IRA?"

He shrugs, but I can tell that I'm right. "Ian has been involved in Peace House for many years now. He first came to us as a volunteer. And then he came again. And again. He said Peace House helped him to find his way out…"

Out of the IRA, I'm thinking. But I don't say this.

"And for the last ten years or so, Ian has been an important benefactor to Peace House. A very generous benefactor."

I nod.

"But there are people who would not take kindly to this information."

I remember the quote from the taxi driver today. "For every Irishman on the fire, there will always be another ready to turn the spit," I say.

He nods. "You understand how some of the Irish think."

"Hopefully it's only a small minority."

"Aye, lassie. And I'm sure it is. But we must look out for one another."

"Thank you for telling me about Ian," I say. I can't believe how relieved I feel right now. Thinking that something was wrong with Ian was really eating at me. And remembering this reminded me of how he mentioned coming to Antrim on the day Ryan's dad was killed.

"Can I ask you one more thing about Ian?"

"You ask, and I will decide if I can answer."

So I ask him about that day, the day Ian's brother and Michael were killed by the bomb.

" 'Twas Ian's second summer here at Peace House," he tells me slowly. " 'Twas driving a load of children up from Belfast that day, Ian was. He'd tried to find another driver to replace him but without luck. Or perhaps 'twas with great luck. Or, more likely, it was the good Lord watching out for one o' his lambs. Driving those children out here 'twas the only reason Ian himself was not killed that day."

"Oh."

"Ian says Peace House saved his life."

I nod, still taking this in. Everything actually adds up. "You told me I can't tell anyone," I say. "Does this include my aunt and Michael's son, Ryan?"

He seems to think about this. "I'm not concerned about your aunt, lassie. But does Ryan have any connection with the IRA?"

I shake my head.

"You're certain o' it?"

I consider this. Ryan seems to know a lot about the IRA as well as the RIRA. But I seriously doubt he has any real connection with them. On the other hand, I remember how he's shown sympathies for their cause from time to time, and knowing the history of his father, well, who can be sure?

"I guess I don't know with absolute certainty," I tell Murphy. "So I promise not to tell Ryan about any of this unless I am one hundred percent sure."

"Thank you, lassie. I'm sure you wouldn't want Ian's blood on your hands."

I feel my eyes open wide. "No," I say quickly, "of course not."

For the second time, I thank him and tell him I should go. And, once again, he reminds me of the need to be discreet.

"For Ian's sake," he says as he shakes my hand.

I nod. "For Ian's sake."

As I retrace my steps back toward Peace House, I feel torn. On one hand, I have permission to tell my aunt, but what will this information do to her? On the other hand, I'm not supposed to tell Ryan, but he's the one who really needs to know. What am I supposed to do?

And so, as I walk, I ask God to help me figure this out.

Seventeen

hat's up?" Ryan asks when I find him sitting on a stone bench outside of Peace House.

"Didn't you go out on the lake?" I ask as I sit down beside him.

"The boats were all being used," he says.

"Oh."

"So, did you meet the old dude? Did you ask him about Ian?"

I'm trying to decide how to answer him when my aunt walks up.

"Hey, you two," she says, "I just finished my interview."

"How did it go?" I ask, standing up to meet her.

"Great. I think I can complete my article now."

"With a happy ending?" I ask.

She smiles. "For the most part. And then I can use a separate article to tell the rest of the story."

"So, are you ready to go?" I ask, thinking this will be a good distraction from the conversation I'm trying to avoid with Ryan.

"Actually, I thought we'd spend the night," she says. "They have rooms for rent upstairs."

"Cool," says Ryan. "Maybe I'll get to take a boat out later. They said they're all available after five today."

"Well, why don't we just stick around and enjoy the place

then?" she says. "Maybe I can get some photos while the light is still good."

"Want me to get the bags out of the car?" Ryan offers.

"Thanks," says Sid. "I'll go check us in." She glances at me. "Why don't you come along and get the keys for Ryan?"

So I follow Sid back into the office and wait as she makes arrangements with Glenda.

"Did you have tea with Murphy?" Glenda asks as she hands us the keys.

"Yes," I answer, wishing she hadn't said anything.

"Murphy, the old groundskeeper?" asks Sid.

"That'd be the one," says Glenda.

"I can't believe he's still here."

Glenda nods, then turns her attention back to me. "Was he able to answer your questions, dear?"

"Yes. We had a nice chat," I say. "I'll run these keys to Ryan, Sid."

"Great. Let's meet up again at dinnertime."

"There's a separate dining room for guests," Glenda starts telling us before I can leave. "Just to the right of the main dining hall. But you're welcome to eat with the children if you like. Just be warned: it can be a bit noisy in there."

"Would it be okay if I took some photos of the children?" my aunt asks.

Glenda hands her a form. "You'll need permission if you want to use photos for any publication." When she starts explaining how to fill out the form, I make a quick getaway. Hopefully Sid will be distracted enough to forget about my conversation with Murphy.

Ryan has already unloaded the bags, and I help him carry them back into the building. Our rooms are on the second floor, but we noticed the service elevator, located in the back of the building, in our earlier exploration. As we ride the elevator, I tell him about the dining hall and the separate place for adult guests, taking more time than necessary to explain these details, filling up all the empty spaces in our conversation lest he ask me about Murphy again. Then, to my relief, we are standing outside of our rooms.

"I'll put Sid's things in her room," he tells me, and I drop the things I was carrying for her on the floor.

"Thanks," I say as I rebalance my stuff and go into my room, shutting the door behind me. I'm out of breath and can hardly believe I made it here without telling the news about Ian to anyone. Neither my aunt or Ryan. Whew.

Okay, I tell myself as I dump my biggest bag on the floor, Ryan is *not* a member of the IRA. That's totally ridiculous. Even if he is slightly sympathetic to the republic's cause, he would never consider joining their ranks. Besides, I remind myself, the IRA is almost nonexistent now anyway. And Ryan, like Sid and me, knows that the RIRA is bad news. I'm sure he has absolutely no sympathy toward them. So why am I being so paranoid? Then I remember Murphy's concern and the way he mentioned Ian's blood on my hands. Maybe I do need to be careful.

So I decide to lay low for the evening. I'll make sure I'm not around Ryan by myself. And, okay, this is kind of a bummer since

I've grown to really like this guy and wouldn't mind spending more time with him. And I think maybe he likes me. I mean, beyond just being happy traveling companions that my aunt has thrown together. And I'm well aware that our time in Ireland will soon be over. Don't think about it, I tell myself.

So, to distract myself, I play my penny flute for a while. And then I write in my journal. After that, I read a little from an Irish novel I picked up in Belfast. But the story is so depressing that I realize it's not helping my state of mind at all. Finally I decide to wander downstairs and see if there's something I can do to occupy myself until dinner, hopefully something that won't involve Ryan or my aunt.

"So, are you guys sticking around then?" says the red-headed guy we met down by the lake. He's carrying a small box through the lobby.

"Yeah. Just for the night," I tell him.

"I'm Stewart," he tells me, shifting the box with one hand as he sticks out the other to shake mine. "I'm from New Jersey."

"Maddie," I say. "From Washington State."

"So what brings you here?"

I explain how my aunt was a volunteer here during the troubles and how she's writing a follow-up article now. "This is such a cool place," I tell him. "I might even look into volunteering here myself. Maybe next summer."

"Cool." He gets an I-have-an-idea look. "If you'd like a taste of what it's really like to work here, I've heard they're short-handed in the kitchen this week. One of the girls has tonsillitis."

"Really?"

He nods. "You interested in giving it a go?"

"Sure, why not?"

So he walks me back to the kitchen and introduces me to Megan, the kitchen boss, a woman in her thirties. She gives me a quick tour, then hands me an apron and a peeler, and soon I find myself standing over a big stainless-steel bowl of potatoes. Okay, it's not exactly glamorous, but it's the perfect escape from this Ian dilemma with Ryan and Sid.

Megan seems pleased with my work and even more pleased when I offer to help with the serving as well as the cleanup later tonight. "Can you stay for the whole summer?" she asks in a pleading voice.

"Sorry," I tell her. "But maybe I can help you with breakfast tomorrow."

"Hey, I'll take anything I can get."

I let Sid and Ryan know what's up with me and KP. They look at me like I'm a little crazy, but that's fine. It buys me time. But somewhere between dinner and dessert, Ryan catches me as I'm carrying a tub of dirty silverware back into the kitchen.

"Hey, are you going to tell me about your little talk with Murphy or what?"

"Later," I call over my shoulder. "I'm kinda busy at the moment."

He seems to buy this, and I manage to keep myself "busy" for another couple of hours. Finally Megan tells me that I've worked harder than anyone on kitchen crew and that if I really want to volunteer here next summer, she will personally recommend me for the job.

"Thanks," I tell her.

"Thank you!"

I hang up my apron and take the back staircase to the second floor. I'm practically tiptoeing to my room in fear that I'll run into Ryan and he'll demand to know everything about my conversation with Murphy. Somehow I make it to my room, take a nice long shower to remove all the layers of kitchen scum, and then crawl into bed. It's only eight thirty, but I feel like I've just put in a long day at the farm. Before I turn off my light, I make sure to set my alarm for six. Prep work for breakfast begins at six thirty, and I don't want to be late.

Peace House is much quieter than our last hotel in downtown Belfast, and as a result I sleep soundly and nearly jump out of my skin when the alarm goes off in the morning. It takes me a few minutes to get my bearings and wake myself up, but I'm back down in the kitchen and ready to go by 6:27.

"You're early," says Megan as I grab an apron.

I grin at her. "I'd say it was from growing up on the farm, but the truth is, I'm not that much of a morning person. Although I have been getting up earlier than usual here in Ireland."

"Good that someone is." She shakes her head. "Most of my kitchen crew seem to be coming in later and later. It's about time I gave them the 'talk.'"

She puts me to work cracking dozens of eggs into a big aluminum bowl. Before long the rest of her crew stumble in. They look a little bleary-eyed, and I notice some of their eyes are bloodshot.

"Looks like they've been hitting the Guinness again," she tells me in a hushed tone. "Glad you could make it, people," she says more loudly, then starts assigning jobs.

I find it surprising that the camp staff would be out drinking, but then I remember that I'm in Ireland, and while peace camps have a light Christian influence (they pray before their meals), it's nothing like the Christian camps I attended as a kid. Anyone caught with alcohol at those camps would've been in serious trouble.

The focus here is more on people and accepting differences and living in peace with one another. I can tell by conversations I've picked up on with the kitchen crew that they aren't exactly Christians. I mean, they're not bad people, and they are volunteering their time. But I can tell some of them have issues. Still, I think it's cool to be here. And if I do come back next summer, I hope my walk with God is a little stronger than it seems now. Although, curiously enough, I feel like it's getting stronger each day. I'm not sure why. Maybe it's because I'm praying more.

As I move from task to task in the kitchen, I begin to strategize a way that might allow both my aunt and Ryan to find out the truth about Ian. I get so obsessed with my plan that I almost don't notice my arm's getting sore as I stir a big bowl of pancake batter. (Megan's big mixer is on the blink.) I start stirring with my left hand and say a silent prayer that God will help this crazy plan to work.

Finally breakfast is served and cleaned up, and my job in the kitchen comes to an end. Megan thanks me again and reminds me that she'd be happy to have me on her kitchen crew anytime. And I promise to keep that in mind.

It's almost ten by the time I find my aunt and Ryan. They're downstairs in the lobby, discussing their plans for the day.

"I thought I might write for a couple of hours," she tells us. "Then we can head out and grab some lunch in Antrim before we shoot on down to Dublin."

"Why Dublin?" I ask, thinking this throws a significant wrench into the plan I've been concocting all morning.

"Why not?" She looks at me.

"Do you have an interview down there or something?"

"No, but I thought you two might enjoy seeing it."

I glance at Ryan now, hoping he'll support me in this. "I was thinking it'd be cool to head back toward Malin," I tell her.

"Malin?" One of her brows lifts slightly. "Why?"

"Well, it's where Ryan's family came from, and he barely got to meet his aunt, and he might want to get to know her better. And I actually had a really good time there. Besides that, I've heard that Dublin is a really big, busy city. And, well, Belfast was like that. I guess I just prefer the quiet Irish countryside."

"Really?" Sid doesn't look convinced.

I toss Ryan a glance now. Like, *Hint, hint, help me out here.*

"I wouldn't mind going back to Malin," he says. "I was sort of wishing I'd done that bike trip around Malin Head like Maddie did. It sounded pretty cool."

Sid considers this. "Yeah, I was sort of wishing I'd done that too."

"And Malin's on the way to Galway," I point out. "It's not like it would take any more time to go that way."

"No." She nods as if she's getting into this. "Actually, it would probably take less. To be honest, I'm not that crazy about driving through the big cities either. But are you sure you guys are okay with this?"

"Better than okay," I assure her.

"I think it's a good plan," Ryan adds. "I like the idea of going back to a place I'm sort of familiar with. It's kind of like going home."

"And Malin is kind of like home," I say. "I mean, it's your ancestors' home."

So it seems to be settled. Sid heads up to her room for some writing time, and then Ryan confronts me. "What's up, Maddie?"

"I can't tell you just yet."

"Does Malin have anything to do with whatever this is you're not telling me yet?"

"Sort of." Now I realize I'll need Ryan's help to accomplish this crazy plan, so I have to divulge a little more. "It also involves Derry and a certain restaurant there."

"And Ian too?"

I nod. "Listen, Ryan, if you help me pull this off, I promise to explain it all later. Okay?"

He nods. "I'm in."

"We need to look at a map."

Ryan produces a small fold-up map from his pocket. "Will this do?"

"Perfect." I point to where we are now. "It looks like it could take about an hour and a half to get to Derry," I tell him.

"That sounds about right."

"But I want us to get there around dinnertime."

"We'd have to hang out in Antrim until four or later. That's a pretty long lunch, Maddie."

"I know. So we need to find some place along the way where we can kill some time. A castle or something. Something we're both *dying* to see. We stop there and manage to spend a couple of hours or even more so we arrive in Derry around six or seven. By then we are both *starving* for dinner and can't wait until we reach Malin to eat. Then we'll discreetly direct Sid to Ian's restaurant, like, 'Hey, why don't we eat there?' She has no idea of the name of Ian's restaurant. And then, of course, she will have to meet with him."

"What if he's not there?" he asks.

"I'll call ahead and make sure that he is."

"What if he doesn't want to see Sid?"

"I'll admit I thought that could be the case. I mean, he never mentioned her or anything while we were in Malin. But I got to thinking that she's the one who refused to see him in the first place. So maybe it's his pride—you know, the male ego thing."

"Are you suggesting that women don't have egos?"

"You know what I mean, Ryan. Anyway, what if Ian thought Sid should've come to meet him that day in Malin? What if her not coming hurt his feelings? If you think about it, it must've seemed odd to him, after all those years, that she wouldn't even pop in to say hey. If he felt bad, he might have acted like he didn't care."

"Or maybe he really didn't care."

"How will we ever know?"

"But what if it's a big mistake for them to meet?"

"It might be," I admit. "But if that's the case, it might be good for Sid's sake to get this whole thing over with. Then she can go home and get on with her life. It's obvious she's been kind of stuck. You heard the conversation with your mom, Ryan. You're the one who told me she was heartbroken over Ian."

"Well, I'll do what I can to help you, Maddie. But then you have to tell me about this mysterious conversation with Murphy. It must've reflected pretty well on Ian, or you wouldn't be going to all this trouble."

I study him for a moment. Why don't I just tell him everything now? Get it over with, out in the open. But then I remember my promise to Murphy. "I'd rather wait, Ryan. I need to talk to Ian first. Okay?"

"Yeah. Whatever."

I can tell Ryan's a little offended by my secrecy. But, really, what else can I do? At least he seems willing to play along. Even better, I don't have to keep avoiding him now. That's a relief. Consequently, when he invites me to go for a boat ride with him, I happily accept. I just hope he doesn't threaten to drown me if I don't tell him what Murphy said.

Eighteen

Ryan and I take turns rowing the small boat, but he is a lot better at it. Of course, my excuse is that my arms are tired from stirring all that pancake batter this morning. Fortunately, he doesn't seem to mind. I tell myself it's a guy thing. And it suits me fine. I'm enjoying just lazing around in the front of the boat, watching him sweat. Okay, he's not really sweating. It's actually cooled off a bit today, and I wish I'd brought a sweater. Finally he informs me that it's nearly noon and maybe we should head back to check on Sid.

"No hurry," I tell him as he swiftly begins to paddle us toward the dock.

"Oh, yeah," he says, pausing to take a break. "I guess you're right." He leans his head back and looks up at the sky that's dappled with clouds, and he slowly gazes around the lake as if he's trying to take in all this incredible Irish scenery. Finally he looks over at me and smiles. "You really do look like you belong here, Maddie."

"Huh?" I sit up straighter.

"You look like you could be Irish."

I can't help but smile. "Is that a compliment?"

He nods with a slight twinkle in his eye. "And, just like the Irish, you've decided to become irritatingly mysterious too."

So I try to give him a coy little sideways glance—my best attempt at looking *mysterious.* But he just laughs and resumes his rowing.

Ryan and I take our time loading the car with our stuff, and then I add an unplanned stall tactic when I realize I actually left my backpack in the lobby when I was getting volunteer information to take home.

"We're burning daylight," my aunt warns me as I come walking back to the car.

"Sorry," I tell her, acting like I'm hurrying to get in. I glance at my watch as she drives away from Peace House. It's already close to one, and we're not even to Antrim yet. So far so good.

Sid makes good time getting into town. She impatiently looks for a place to park and then hurries to get out and lock the car, acting like she's running late. Even after we get seated in the pub, she seems worried about the time. That's when I remind her that her work is done now and it's time to relax and hang loose. "Enjoy some downtime," I tell her as the waiter appears.

We order our food, and when he asks what we'll have to drink, I surprise both of them, as well as myself, by ordering a pint of Guinness.

"Maddie?" My aunt stares at me with her head slightly cocked.

"May I see your identification, miss?"

I reach for my bag, extract my passport, and proudly present the document to the waiter.

"Thank you." He examines it and hands it back.

"I'll have a Guinness too," says Ryan. But he gives me a curious sideways glance as he produces his ID for the waiter.

"Same for me," says my aunt, still staring at me. "What's going on here?" she asks me as soon as the waiter departs.

I just shrug. "Hey, when in Rome…"

"But I thought you said it was against your Christian values," she reminds me. "Or something to that effect."

"Yeah," says Ryan in a slightly accusing tone. "I hope you're not tossing aside your own convictions about alcohol because you think it will please us."

"To be honest, I'm not sure whether I was espousing my personal convictions or just parroting what my parents believe. If anything, this trip has shown me that I can be a little too quick to judge others. I need to learn to think and discern for myself."

"But, Maddie—"

"It's my decision," I tell my aunt. "And besides, I'm curious what Guinness tastes like. And this is Ireland. I can't very well go home without giving it a try, can I?"

"And I guess you can't become an alky in just three days," Ryan points out with a teasing smile.

As it turns out, I'm not overly thrilled with the taste of stout. It's strong and bitter, and I think it smells a little like fish. But I don't want to reveal my true opinions to Ryan or my aunt. I'm pretty sure they'd laugh at me. So, between bites of food, I somehow force down about a third of my pint.

"Not much of a stout drinker after all?" Ryan teases me as I stand up to excuse myself. But instead of stopping at the rest room like I told them, I go out behind the pub to make a phone call to Ian's restaurant. I study the card for Ian's restaurant. The name of the restaurant sounds kind of French, which I think is odd. But then I suppose the Irish might enjoy French cuisine as much as Americans do. I look for the phone number and carefully dial. I figure I'll have a better chance of catching him during the middle of the day like this, but what if he's taken the day off? I actually shoot up a quick prayer as I listen to the phone ring. To my pleasant surprise, it's Ian who answers.

"Chez Marsilius. This is Ian."

I clear my throat and tell him who I am and that we might be in Derry around dinnertime tonight. "Should we make reservations?" I ask. "I mean, I'm not sure when we'll get there, but I'm thinking between six and seven."

"I'll have a table ready," he tells me. "How many should I expect?"

Okay, it could be my imagination, but I think I can hear curiosity in his voice when he asks about the number. "Three," I tell him. "My aunt will be with Ryan and me."

"Very good," he says, sounding professional, just like the proprietor of a restaurant.

"Unless you'd like to join us," I add.

There's a brief pause, and I wonder if I've overstepped my bounds again. "I mean, you might be busy or—"

"No," he says slowly. "That might be a good idea, Maddie. I'll have them set the table for four."

"Cool."

He kind of laughs. "Yes, *cool*."

I ask him for directions, and it sounds like the place is easy to find. Even so, I make some notes on the back of his card.

I try to conceal my excitement when I return to the table, but when Sid's not looking, I give Ryan a thumbs-up. Good to go.

"Do you want to finish your Guinness before we go?" Ryan asks.

I'm not sure if it's a stall tactic or a challenge to me, but I turn my nose up at it. "Not so much."

"Just admit it, Maddie," he persists. "You don't like it, do you?"

I shrug as my aunt pays the bill. "I guess it's an acquired taste."

"Maddie, you certainly don't have to drink Guinness just because we do," my aunt says as we leave the pub. "And you really shouldn't drink it at all if it compromises what you believe. I sure don't want your parents blaming me for corrupting you in Ireland."

Sid seems more relaxed when we get back in the car. I think she's taken our advice. But after we've driven for nearly forty minutes, I start getting worried. So far I haven't seen one single thing that provides a believable excuse for a quick detour. Finally I spot a sign for a pottery factory that's about ten miles off the main highway. Yeah, that should work, especially since Sid likes Irish pottery.

"Hey, Sid, how about we check that pottery place out?" I reach over her shoulder and point to the sign on the left.

"I didn't know you liked pottery," she says.

"I want to get Mom something," I say.

"And I wouldn't mind getting something too," Ryan adds. "To remember this trip by. Maybe a bowl or something…"

"All right," says Sid as she makes the turn. "You won't hear me arguing. I'd love to find a few more pieces."

It turns out that it's more than just a pottery factory. The place is run by monks, and they also make goat cheese and weave wool and do all sorts of things. Ryan and I pretend to be interested in everything, and before I know it, I actually am interested. When Sid's not looking, I give Ryan the directions to Ian's restaurant. I figure with him in the front seat, it'll be more believable if he navigates us there.

Finally it's nearly five o'clock, and Sid insists we should finish up our visit here. "This place is great," she says, "but I really don't like driving in Ireland after dark." Naturally, we don't argue. It's about five thirty by the time we're actually back on the highway again. And, because of the hour, there are more cars, and the traffic moves slower. Perfect. So it is that we come into Derry at about a quarter of seven.

"I'm starving," Ryan says.

"Me too," I echo, feeling like a six-year-old.

"I'm not that familiar with places in Derry," she says. "But that looks like a good possi—"

"How about that street?" says Ryan quickly, pointing to a street that Ian mentioned to me.

"Okay." My aunt turns into the roundabout, then takes the left turn out. "Now where?"

"I don't know," says Ryan. "But it looks like this is a good area." So she drives down the fairly busy street, suggesting several places, but between Ryan and me, we manage to dissuade her.

"That place looks interesting," says Ryan, pointing to the right.

"Chez Marsilius," I say, hoping I got the name right. "Sounds French. Hey, that'd be fun."

"French?" Sid sounds unconvinced.

"Yeah," says Ryan. "I've heard there's an Irish-French connection. Maybe we should check it out."

So she finds a place to park, and we slowly walk back toward the restaurant. "It looks pretty nice," she says. "Do you think we're dressed well enough?"

"This is summer," I remind her. "And Ireland is used to tourists. Once they see we're Americans, they might cut us some slack."

"I hope so."

We go inside, and it's obvious this is a very nice place. Fresh flowers, candlelight, and white tablecloths. I toss Ryan a look.

"Maybe Sid and I should go freshen up," I say quickly. "Why don't you see if you can get us a table?" Then I turn to Sid. "You might want to check your hair," I suggest. "It's kind of windblown."

"Good idea." She nods as she pats her hair. "It's bad enough to be dressed so casually. No sense in looking like total hicks."

So we go to what turns out to be a very nice ladies' room, where Sid fixes her hair, checks her makeup, and even puts on a scarf. "There," she says to me. "Do you think they'll let me in now?"

I smile. "Yeah. I just hope I can pass too."

"You're a teenager," she reminds me. "No one expects you to look good."

"Thanks a lot!"

She laughs, and we go back to the foyer, but I spot Ryan

already seated at a nice table by a fireplace. "There's Ryan," I whisper to Sid. And we both go in to join him.

Okay, my heart is pounding like a jackhammer. My palms are sweaty, and I'm sure I won't be able to eat a thing. I'm walking ahead of Sid, amazed I can travel in a straight line because of how bad my knees are shaking. Seriously, if I get so unraveled doing something like this, how hopeless would I be working for something like the IRA? Okay, flush that thought.

I smile at Ryan. "Everything okay?" I ask in a tight-sounding voice that I'm sure must be a dead giveaway to my aunt.

"Groovy," he says as he gets up to pull out Sid's chair for her.

I pull out my own and slowly sit down, telling myself to chill. And breathe.

"Why are there four places?" Sid asks casually. If she suspects anything, she's hiding it well.

I kind of shrug. But then I see her face. Her smile has completely evaporated, and it's obvious she's looking at something extremely disturbing. Something that's directly behind me. For all I can tell the wall's about to fall on us. Her eyes are huge, and I swear I can see her nostrils flaring.

"What is going on?" she hisses at me.

"What do you—"

Before I can finish, she is on her feet and heading straight out of here.

"We'll be back," I say to Ryan. Then I follow her, assuming she's heading back to the ladies' room. But when I see the back of her, practically running, she is going right out the door. Great.

I sprint after her, catching her on the sidewalk, a few doors down and nearly to the car. Like what's she going to do? Jump in the car and drive off without us? Strand us here in Derry? Maybe.

She gets into her car, and when I try to open the passenger side, it is locked. Now I'm starting to freak. I mean, I know that Sid hasn't been herself when certain things have happened—things related to Ian. But what if she has a meltdown right here in the street? I mean, she's not that old, but she could have a stroke or something.

I lean over and knock on the window, signaling her to let me in. But she doesn't even turn to look. Okay, this is serious.

Dear God, I pray silently but desperately, *please, please help me. I love Sid, and I don't want to hurt her. If I've done something wrong, I'm really, really sorry. But please help me fix this, for her sake. Please!*

I bend over and look inside the car again. Sid's head is leaning against the steering wheel. Is she conscious? I tap on the window again, this time more quietly. And finally, after what feels like five minutes, she turns and looks at me. Okay, she's glaring at me. But she does unlock the door.

As I get in, I wonder if I might not be safer on the outside. Still, I started this thing; I guess I'd better finish it. "Sid," I begin in my most gentle voice, "I'm sorry I—"

"Madison!" she yells at me, turning to look me in the eyes. "I cannot believe you! What on earth do you think you're doing? I told you as clearly as I could that I did not want anything to do with that, that person. And you obviously set this whole thing up just so you could—"

"Let me explain," I try to cut in.

"No!" she screams. "Let *me* explain!"

I shrink back into the seat.

She holds her hands out as if she's trying to keep a lid on something. "Okay, let me calm down first." She takes a deep breath. "I'm sure you didn't realize what you were getting into, Maddie," she continues in a much calmer voice. "You probably thought, 'Oh, this is so romantic, I think I'll play matchmaker.'" She turns and narrows her eyes at me. "Right?"

"Sort of."

"Wrong!" she shouts. Then she calms herself again. "Sorry…I'm the grownup here. I'll try to act like it." She turns around in her seat and gives me a fake smile. "Okay, Maddie, it's like this. Yes, I was in love with Ian—a long, long time ago. And Ian might have been in love with me. But he was also in love with his Irish republic, and he was in love with the IRA. And when I realized he was unable to give that up for me, I broke it off with him." She snaps her fingers. "And, just like that, it was over. Finished. Done."

"But, Sid—"

"No buts, Maddie. There is absolutely nothing I have to say to Ian McMahan, and I seriously doubt he has anything to say to me. I can't believe he even agreed to meet here with me."

"Ian has changed, Sid."

"We've all changed, Maddie. Now if you would get yourself back into that overly priced French restaurant and retrieve your little partner in crime, we'll be on our way."

"But, Sid—"

"I said no buts."

"Okay," I tell her. "You made me listen to you. But could you at least listen to me?"

"Do I have to?"

I consider this. "Well, I suppose you could dump Ryan and me here in Derry and just leave us in Ireland. Of course, you'd have to explain to my parents what happened, and I'm sure—"

"Fine," she snaps. "Make it brief."

"Ian isn't in the IRA," I tell her, and before she can interrupt— and I know she wants to—I continue. "That's why he wasn't with Ryan's dad the day the bomb went off."

She just shakes her head with a sour expression.

"Would you like to hear where Ian was that day?" I ask, hoping she'll take the bait, but she just shrugs. "Fine, I'll tell you anyway. *He was taking a load of kids to Peace House.*"

"Who told you that?" Her eyes are narrow, and I can tell she doesn't believe me.

"Murphy."

"Murphy, the groundskeeper at Peace House?"

"That's the one."

I can tell she still doesn't believe me. "Really, Maddie. Why would you have a conversation like that with Murphy? And, even if you did, how would you know if the old guy's senile or not? Good grief, he must be about a hundred by now."

"He's not senile." Then I tell her about the photo I saw and how Glenda at the front desk suggested I speak to Murphy. "He told me the whole story, Sid. And he told me not to tell anyone."

"Why not?"

"Because it could put Ian in danger."

She makes a humph sound, like she's still not convinced.

"Ian is a benefactor to the camp, Sid. He contributes a lot."

She actually rolls her eyes now. "Ian McMahan? The man was poor as a church mouse when I knew him."

"Like you said, it's been a long time. People change." Then I remember something. "You seemed impressed with the restaurant."

"Yeah, I'm sure Ian planned to stick us with a big bill too."

"Ian owns the restaurant."

"I don't believe it."

"It's easy to prove. He gave me his business card, except Ryan has it right now."

"Fine. Ian owns a restaurant. That still doesn't change anything."

"But he left the IRA. He helps out at Peace House."

"But no one's supposed to know." She makes a face. "Yeah, right."

"Murphy said it was for Ian's protection, that if his old IRA connections found out, well, you know how they can be. Remember what the cab driver said about one Irishman on the fire and the other turning the spit?"

She just shakes her head and then leans it against the steering wheel again.

"He's changed, Sid."

She lets out a long, low groan now. Like an animal in pain.

"Can't you just talk to him? Like a civilized adult? Bury the hatchet?"

Another groan.

"Sid, what can it hurt?"

Slowly she sits up, and when she turns to look at me, I can see tears glistening in her eyes. "What can it hurt?" she asks in a quiet but shaky voice. "Tell me, Maddie, have you ever had your heart broken?"

I consider this. "I felt pretty bad when Ross Hardwick didn't ask me to the prom."

"That's not the same."

"Sorry."

"If you'd had your heart broken, Maddie, you wouldn't ask, what can it hurt? You would know."

I let out a long sigh now. "I don't know what to do."

"Me neither."

"What do you think Danielle would tell you to do?"

"Run for my life."

"Seriously, Sid. Danielle married Michael."

"And look where that got her."

"But she must've loved him enough to take a risk. Now no one is asking you to marry Ian, but it seems you could at least go in and have a civilized conversation with him."

"Why?"

"Why not?" I'm feeling a tiny bit of hope now, like maybe she's finally softening. "He's a nice guy, Sid. And he's interesting. And I bet you could use some of what he's been through for your article. I mean, he's totally reformed from being a member of the IRA to being a benefactor to Peace House. Kind of like the counterpart to the guy in your first interview, the bomber dude."

"Sean Potter."

"Yeah. Kind of a juxtaposition, if you will."

This actually makes her chuckle. "When did you get so smart, Maddie?"

"Maybe I'm learning from you."

"Okay, maybe you're right. Maybe I am overreacting. And I suppose a conversation with Ian McMahan might be interesting. For my article, I mean."

I nod with enthusiasm. "Yes, for your article."

She turns on the light in her car now, checks herself out in the rearview mirror, then touches up her lipstick, and looks at me. "Am I okay?"

"You're beautiful."

"Well, you don't have to go overboard."

"This is going to be good," I assure her as we get out of the car. "You're going to be glad you did this."

"I doubt it. But maybe the food will be good."

"And it's on the house," I tell her as we get to the entrance.

"Well, I'll be sure to order the works then."

I open the door for her, but she stalls, and I'm afraid she's going to bolt again, maybe for good this time. "Come on," I tell her. "You can do this."

"What makes you think so?"

I pat her on the back. "Because you're my role model, Aunt Sid, and I'd like to think that if you can do this, I can do all kinds of things."

"You ever think of practicing law, Maddie?"

I laugh as we walk through the foyer.

"You have to promise to help me out in there," she whispers as we head back toward the table.

"I'm here for you."

When we reach the table, Sid pastes a big (okay, slightly phony) smile on her face as she reaches for Ian's hand. "Ian McMahan, it's been so long. How have you been anyway?"

He stands now and takes her hand as a somewhat shy smile barely turns up the corners of his mouth. "I'm doing well, Sidney. And you are looking as lovely as ever."

Her smile grows more genuine. "I'm sorry to run out on you like that, but I remembered something I had to take care of." She holds up her hands. "You know how it is being a busy journalist. Always getting calls from the home office, new assignments, stories breaking."

"You're a journalist?" he says with interest. "I'm sure you must be a very good one."

And on it goes. The two of them chatting away like old friends. Okay, I'm thinking perhaps they both have a bit of the blarney in them. Perhaps Sid more than Ian. But as the evening progresses, I relax a little. And Ryan seems amused by their conversation. And the food is fantastic!

"Would you like to have dessert in a private room?" Ian asks as we come to the end of our meal. "Then we could all speak more freely."

Sid's brows lift a bit. "That sounds nice."

Ian nods to a waiter and then escorts us to a room off the back. It's very elegant with more candlelight and another fireplace that's already burning. A table full of a selection of desserts is already set up, along with coffee, tea, and some kind of after-dinner wine.

"Looks like someone was expecting us," says Sid as she slides into a big, comfortable chair.

"This is nice," I observe.

"It's a room we use for dignitaries," he says.

"Well, I feel special," says Sid in a teasing voice.

Then Ian asks us what we'd like and acts as our waiter as he brings us dessert and coffee, then finally sits down to join us.

"I thought you might have some questions," Ian begins, "and that we might all be more comfortable with a private setting."

"Maddie has already filled me in some," Sid says, giving me a look that I think must be a hint. "She spoke to someone at the peace camp about you."

"Peace House?" His brow creases slightly.

"Yes," I say quickly. "I noticed a photograph of you there, and I asked Murphy some questions."

"You spoke to Murphy?" Ian looks surprised.

I nod. "He's really nice. And for some reason he trusted me. I told him a little about my aunt and Ryan's dad and stuff. And then I asked him about you. I hope you don't mind, but he told me about your involvement with Peace House."

I can tell Ian doesn't really want to talk about this, but I explain how Ryan was having a hard time accepting Ian's role in his dad's death. "Neither one of us could figure out why you didn't drive him to the airport that day," I finally say, just laying my cards on the table. "It was suspicious. He was killed, but you weren't. Can you see what I mean?" I glance over at Ryan, and he seems relieved that I brought this up.

Ian nods slowly. "Yes. I guess I never looked at it like that. I always figured everyone would know how upset I was to lose both a brother and a friend that day. And I suppose I blamed myself too. I thought maybe if I had been driving, well, things would've gone differently. I ran it through my head over and over."

"Ryan doesn't know why you weren't driving that day," I say.

So Ian tells us all about how he'd been getting involved in the peace camp. "It was your aunt's influence," he tells me. "She'd been very committed to it, and after she left—and I realized all that I'd lost—well, I looked into helping out myself." He looks at Sid now. "It was amazing. When I started working with the kids, getting to know them one on one, I felt things changing inside of me. It's as if the children helped me to heal. And finally I realized I had to cut all ties to the IRA. I'd been working on doing just that when Michael came back. And although I spent time with him, I felt torn. I'd already committed to transport those children from Belfast to Peace House even though the dates for the transports hadn't been nailed down. Just the same, I felt I had to stick to that commitment, especially when I couldn't find anyone to do it for me." He sadly shakes his head. "And then…well, you know what happened."

Ryan nods now. "Thanks for telling me, Ian. It makes sense."

"As broken up as I was over what happened that day," he continues, "it sealed the deal for me. I knew I would never go back."

We talk and talk, finally moving on to lighter topics. Ian tells
us how he spent some time in France and how much he enjoyed
their food. "And I met Jean Marsilius and enticed him to come
back and help me start this restaurant." He waves his hand. "That
was about seventeen years ago."

"It's a beautiful restaurant," Sid tells him.

"Thank you."

I'm not sure if it's the candlelight or what, but their eyes seem
to be glowing, and the atmosphere has definitely warmed up in
here, and I'm not talking about the fireplace.

"Goodness," says Sid. "It's so late, and we still have to drive to
Malin."

"Do you have more interviews?" he asks.

"No, it was just our destination."

"Oh." He nods.

"Why don't we spend the night in Derry?" I suggest.

"Yeah," says Ryan. "You don't like to drive at night anyway, Sid."

"There are good hotels nearby," Ian offers, "and lots of good
sights to see in Derry County."

So that settles it. We thank Ian for a lovely dinner, and he calls
ahead and makes a reservation at a hotel that's only three blocks
away. "My friend William runs this place," he tells Sid. "I think
you will be pleased."

His friend's place turns out to be perfect. Not one of the huge, impersonal hotels but still with all the bells and whistles. Not only that, but his friend gives us the "friends' discount," which pleases Sid.

Sid and I share a room again. "Thanks, Maddie," she tells me before we go to sleep. "For everything."

And before I go to sleep, I thank God for working this thing out. Okay, I realize that Sid and Ian aren't falling madly in love or getting married or anything. At least not that I know of. But they didn't kill each other either.

Nineteen

After two delightful days in Derry, with Ian as our devoted guide, we had to part ways this morning in order to make it down to Galway and Shannon Airport in time for our flight home. Ian and Sid promised to stay in touch through e-mail, and Ryan said he actually caught them kissing last night! But we agreed not to tease her about this.

Now we are flying home, and I can hardly believe it's only been two weeks since we came here. Seriously, I feel like a totally different person.

"You seem pretty relaxed," my aunt observes as she closes her laptop and leans back into the seat.

"Why not?" I say.

She laughs. "Don't you remember how frightened you were on the flight out? I thought I was going to have to ask the flight attendant for a sedative for you."

I shrug. "That was then…"

"Hey, I forgot to tell you I talked to your mom at the airport."

"You did?"

"Yeah. I wanted to make sure she had the adjusted flight schedule."

"Yeah, I figured I'd just call her when we got back into the

States," I tell her. "But she probably appreciated hearing from you. You know how protective she can be."

"I know. That's why I figured I should give her a heads-up, since we'll be a few hours late."

"Thanks."

"I told her how great you were to travel with."

"You did?"

"Sure." Sid smiles. "And I told her I was impressed with what a mature, smart, and thoughtful young woman they had raised."

"You really said that?"

"Why not?"

"Wow, thanks again."

"And I told her I'd probably want to take you on all my trips now."

"That'd be cool."

"Well, your mom wasn't too excited about that. Seems she's been missing you. And your dad too."

I nod. "Yeah, that sounds about right. Dad's probably getting ready to harvest and wants me to drive the combine. Mom probably misses me helping with her garden."

"Oh, it's probably more than that."

"Yeah. The truth is, I miss them too."

Sid glances at Ryan peacefully snoozing across the aisle from us. Just as he was on the way over. Although his mouth is closed at the moment, no slobber drooling down his chin. "You know you're lucky to have them, Maddie."

"My family, you mean?"

She nods and keeps looking at Ryan.

"I know…"

"But I think he's feeling more of a sense of family now."

"I hope so." I take a quick glance to be sure he's really asleep, then lower my voice. "He's a nice guy, Sid. I really like him."

She winks at me, then opens her computer again. "Guess I should keep plugging away on this story."

"The one about the RIRA?"

"Yeah. People need to know about this stuff. They need to remember that just because some papers have been signed and some weapons have been destroyed, it doesn't necessarily mean it's over. It takes a lot of people to make and to keep peace."

I consider this as I open my journal and begin to write. I remember how I was fighting with Ryan and even my aunt at first, arguing with them about whether it was right to drink Guinness. I guess that's how religious wars get started. In the end, I decided it wasn't right for me to drink Guinness. Not because God wrote it out in the heavens, but because it gave me a headache and didn't taste that good. Maybe that was God's way of showing me what's best for me. Or maybe I still need to figure some things out. More important, he showed me I can't tell other people what's best for them.

I think about my friend Katie and how she thought she'd be engaged before I got home. I remember how adamant I was about that being wrong, wrong, wrong. Now I'm not so sure. I guess I'll tell her that she'll have to figure it out for herself. Well, with God's help. I write several more pages and finally end up falling asleep.

"Please prepare for landing," the flight attendant is saying over the loudspeaker. "Please put your tray tables into their upright position. Make sure your seat belts are securely fastened and seats fully upright."

I sit up straight and follow the instructions, thinking how we'll be home soon. Ryan is awake now, and he smiles at me from across the aisle. "Doing okay?" he asks.

"Fine." I smile at him and wish I could think of something else to say. It's hard to believe that after hanging with him for two weeks, this is it. We'll be saying good-bye. I mean, I could give him my phone number, but that seems pretty weird. Still, the idea of parting ways makes me really, really sad. I think he's one of the sweetest guys I know.

"Oh, yeah." My aunt nudges me. "I almost forgot to tell you, Maddie. Your mom can't pick you up at the airport."

"She can't?" I feel my spirits plunging.

"She had something at the church. The flight delay kind of messed that up for her."

"Are you taking me home?" I ask hopefully.

"Sorry. I have to go into the office and figure some things out."

"Well, what then?" I'm suddenly feeling like a discarded piece of baggage—like something someone forgot to pick up.

"While you were turning in your receipts at the airport, I asked Ryan if he had time to give you a lift, and he said no problem. Do you mind?"

I feel my face bursting into a smile. "Not at all." Then I pull my brows together. "Although you could've asked me first."

She nods. "Kind of like you asked me about meeting with Ian?"

"Okay…you got me. We're even now."

"Don't be so sure."

"What?"

"Well, I wasn't kidding when I told your mom I'd like to take you on some more trips, Maddie. It gets old traveling alone. I realize you have school and a life, but what do you think about coming along once in a while?"

"Are you kidding?"

"I'm serious."

"I'd love to!" Okay, I'm imagining Paris, Rome, maybe the Swiss Alps, or even Russia. This could be totally awesome. I can't wait to tell Katie. No more fresh-off-the-farm jokes about me.

"Great!" Her eyes light up. "How do you feel about Papua New Guinea?"

"Papua New Guinea?" I hear the enthusiasm draining from my voice. "Isn't that some third-world country where people still live in the Stone Age?"

She smiles. "It's an amazing country, Maddie. No place like it on the planet. Unfortunately there's an AIDS epidemic brewing there with the potential to mimic what's happened in sub-Saharan Africa. That's what my story will be about."

"Papua New Guinea…" I say the exotic name again, trying to soak this in. "Isn't that near Australia?"

"Yes, it's the largest island in the South Pacific. Think rain-forest jungles and exotic birds and tribal cultures. Very remote and unique. Not many people get to travel to places like that."

"Okay." I think her enthusiasm is catching now. "That might be cool."

And so, as our plane lands at Sea-Tac, I imagine myself in light-colored safari-type clothes, walking through a tropical jungle, trying to read a map and a compass. And, okay, my image is a little fuzzy, but I think it'll come into focus before long.

From Notes from a Spinning Planet— Papua New Guinea

Available February 2007

Some of the passengers on this flight are getting all stoked because their final destination is Honolulu, Hawaii. The rest of us will remain on board this "direct flight" to Sydney, Australia. We're only stopping so that the plane can be refueled for the second leg of our journey. I already told Sid that I'd love to get out just so I could brag to my friends that I'd stepped foot in Honolulu, but she said that would probably be impossible due to security. Still, I think I can *say* I was in Honolulu, even if it was brief and my feet never actually touched the ground. At least I've got a window seat on the left side of the plane, which, according to the flight attendant, should help me get a quick peek at Pearl Harbor right before we land and maybe even Diamond Head after we take off. After that, we'll fly all night and reach Sydney the morning of August 10. And August 9, my twentieth birthday, will be permanently erased from my calendar. Weird.

After a while my Margaret Mead book puts me to sleep. And when I wake up, I can hear the pilot announcing that we're only fifteen minutes from landing. I push up the vinyl window shade and look out in time to see some islands appearing. "It's so beautiful down there," I say to Sid.

"Uh-huh." Her nose is still in her computer.

"You should see how blue the water is," I tell her. "It's so clear I think I can see the bottom of the ocean."

"Uh-huh," she mutters again. Whatever she's reading must be really interesting.

I want to ask a flight attendant to point out Pearl Harbor, but it seems they're already getting into their seats, preparing for the landing. And so I just look and try to figure things out for myself. Too bad I didn't think ahead to get a travel brochure or something. Well, if nothing else, I can say that what little I saw of Hawaii was really beautiful.

It's 1:48 p.m. when we touch down in Honolulu. Hawaii time, that is, which I understand is three hours earlier than Pacific Standard Time. Still, I don't readjust my watch yet. Why bother? I observe some of the other passengers standing up and cramming themselves into the narrow aisles as they pry pieces of luggage out of the overhead bins. It's actually kind of funny. Like, what's the hurry since the doors aren't even open yet? But they eagerly stand there with their bags and purses and briefcases and things, just waiting. It reminds me of our cows back home when it's close to feeding time. They'll just line up and wait and wait. Sometimes they'll wait a couple of hours. Finally the passengers begin slowly moving toward the exit. They still remind me of cows as they amble along. It's all I can do to keep myself from mooing as they go past. Or maybe it's just Hawaii envy. I really should grow up.

"You ready?" asks Sid suddenly. Then she closes her laptop and slips it into her briefcase.

"Ready for what?"

"To get off the plane."

"Really?" I say hopefully. "We can get off?"

"Yes," she says. "Didn't you hear the flight attendant say that we can get off here if we want?"

"No." I look around and notice that a lot of passengers are remaining in their seats. But maybe they've stepped foot in Honolulu before.

"I guess you were asleep," she says as we stand up. "I think the plane is going to be here a while. Maybe they need to check something mechanical."

I frown. "Hopefully there's not a problem."

She nods. "Boy, I sure hope not. Oh, yeah, and if we get off, we're supposed to remove our carry-on items too. It's a security thing."

So we both get our carry-on pieces and exit the plane. And I have to admit that it feels so great to stretch my legs, and at least now I can honestly say I've really been in Honolulu, even if it's only the airport. I know Katie will be impressed.

"Hey, do you think I have time to find some postcards?" I ask. "Or do we have to stick around here, close to the plane?"

"I think you have time," she says. "Let's walk this way."

So we walk for what seems quite a ways through the terminal, going past lots of gates, and the next thing I know we've gone right past the security check too. "Aunt Sid," I say suddenly. "We've gone too far! Now we'll have to go through security again."

She laughs. "I don't think so."

"Huh?"

"Happy birthday, Maddie!" She unzips her carry-on and pulls out a slightly rumpled white lei, then puts it around my neck and gives me a big hug. "Aloha, sweetie, and welcome to Honolulu!"

"What?"

"We're staying in Honolulu, Maddie."

"What about Papua New Guinea?" I ask with concern. And, okay, this seems pretty weird, but I'm suddenly worried that *this is it*—that we're not going any farther than Honolulu! And as much as I want to see Hawaii, I don't want to miss going to New Guinea either.

"Oh, don't worry," she tells me. "This is just a little layover. A birthday surprise for you. I didn't really want you to miss your birthday as we flew over the International Date Line."

"Really?"

She nods. "Yes. We have three days to do whatever we please in Honolulu. And then it's back on the plane and off to the other side of the planet." She smiles at me. "So you really do want to go to Papua New Guinea?"

"Of course."

We collect our checked bags and get into a hotel limousine, which takes us to a very cool hotel right along Waikiki.

"Swanky," I say as we go into a very luxurious room that overlooks the beach.

"Swankier than the inn in Clifden, Ireland?" she teases.

I consider this. "You know, they're both swanky in their own way."

She nods. "I'm glad you can appreciate a variety of cultures."

"I'm learning."

She tosses her bags onto one of the queen-size beds and stretches her arms. "Ah, this is just the kind of break I need right now."

"Man, am I glad you told me to pack a swimsuit for this trip," I tell her as I look out the window to see tall palm trees and white sandy beach and miles and miles of varying shades of bright aqua blue water.

"Ready to hit the beach?" she says.

"Woo-hoo!"

We change and gather our beach stuff, then make a quick exodus down to the ocean, where I splash around in the energetic waves, which are surprisingly warm and nothing like the chilly Pacific in Washington State. I even let a couple of friendly guys give me some tips on body surfing, which is way harder than it looks. And finally, feeling totally relaxed and happy, I flop down onto a beach towel next to my aunt and soak up the last rays of afternoon sun.

I could so get used to this!

About the Author

MELODY CARLSON is the award-winning author of more than one hundred books for adults, teens, and children. She is the mother of two grown sons and lives near the Cascade Mountains in central Oregon with her husband and a chocolate Lab retriever. She is a full-time writer and an avid gardener, biker, skier, and hiker.

Coming Spring 2007

Join Maddie Chase on her next international adventure as she explores the beautiful country of Papua New Guinea—and discovers the power of hope.

Available in bookstores and from online retailers.

WATERBROOK PRESS
www.waterbrookpress.com